# STORIES TO POKE YOUR EYES OUT TO

BY

JONATHAN MOON

HOO DOO HEATHENS 2015

Hoo Doo Heathens, Moscow, ID

Cover art and design by Matt Edginton
Edited by Stephanie Gianopoulos

An earlier version of Real Love Burns (STPYEOT Remix) was first published in Houdini Gut Punch, Library of Bizarro Horror Press2010, as Real Love Burns.

Heart of an Angel was originally published in Kizuna: Fiction for
Japan, Brent Millis-2011

Corpse Eater was first published in Undertaker Tales, NorGus Press-2011.

Conversing Doctor DeFeo was first published in Abandoned:
Horror Stories Inside the World of Decaying Madness, Jason Baker-2010

All that Glimmers Isn't Copper was first published in Abandoned
[2], Jason Baker-2010

Poisoned Meat was first published in Thadd Presley Presents:
Horror, Static Movement- 2011

## TABLE OF CONTENTS

# INTRODUCTION

During the final stretch of 2011, Jonathan Moon was suffering from disease, sicker than a scat-hooker. Little to my knowledge, this very same bout of sick was making its way west, and planned to set up shop in my glands as well.

We'd been in touch before, and often held conversation that would later be likened to a couple of juveniles plagued by Tourette's (thank you, Mrs. Moon), and we were quite familiar with each other's work.

There was one time I psychically guessed the nickname his mother used to call him: "Scrappy McAnus Tree." My wife overheard this blithe testimony and downheartedly verified that we were both retarded (thank you, Mrs. Wuchenich). Personally, I thought this display of clairvoyant bravado was impressive, to say the least, but Moon, as he frequently does, burst my bubble by admitting he had no mother. Or father, for that matter, and simply "has always been." I began to think.

One particular day, in the midst of his illness, we were simultaneously chipper and sent a few texts back and forth regarding our oddly optimistic writing plans for the upcoming year. At one point, he was being humorously snide and said something that I knew (or thought I knew, anyway) was what a fallopian tube would say, so I called him out on it. It was the following statement that really made me think twice about continuing any correspondence with him at all, only due to my usual hatred of know-it-alls. But it confirmed my suspicions: Jonathan Moon was a magician who practiced the black arts, and was in league with something far more sinister than even *I* could imagine.

"It's common knowledge that fallopian tubes only make fart noises," he tells me.

I stood aghast and slack-jawed, holding my phone as drool began to puddle within its case. My throat sputtered in intense and patchy quakes as I faced a veil-lifting battle for my soul. My dreams were shattered, and truths were redefined. Within a few seconds, all that I thought I knew, ignited in infinite questions. I began to question first reality, followed closely by my sanity. Both, I led myself to believe, were the testicular moldings of a carnal deity made entirely of Silly Putty.

*Perhaps,* I suddenly thought, *Perhaps Jonathan himself is this Silly Putty god, and it was HE who created my gonad-based perception of what I only imagined truth really was.* Could it be that nothing relevant existed anymore? Life's most basic concepts were turned upside down, and my intellectual essence revealed itself to be nothing more than a theatrical illusion of what I once believed was plausible. But then, everything became clear. Crystal. Crystaaal.

It reaffirmed a fact that I, deep down, believed all along: Moon knew what the fuck he was talking about.

I read his first collection, *Mr. Moon's Nightmares,* in early 2011, and his uninhibited miscreant style resembled the schoolyard misfit with a pocket full of herpes who would sprinkle disease into the cootie-ridden Catholic girls' milk at lunchtime. He was like Dennis the Menace after a satanic séance. His writing was dark and dreary, yet dripping with innocent sorcery. The duality was beyond intriguing and remained consistent throughout the collection. I couldn't wait to see how this six-foot Cthulhuworshiping bastard would evolve.

*The Apocalypse and Satan's Glory Hole* was read soon after, and greedily indulged. I lapped up the dredges of that bitch! This collaboration with Timothy Long produced what could very well be the paramount of bizarro-silly-gore. It's a term that I, literally, just now coined and one that Moon nourished within what could be compared to a grub's lifetime. He deserves nothing less than his own genre. Bizarro-Silly-Gore.

Things always end up in sub-genres, anyways. Nu-metal not included. Because it's dumb. It's not even metal. Anyway ...

Shortly before New Year's, I read his latest opus, the ominous *Heinous*. Sorry, GZA, but Liquid Swords, nothin'. This was liquid *words*. A steadily flowing prose, containing more vivid imagery than krill in the ocean, never grew stale. I found myself constantly chanting, "How do his ideas keep COMING?"

Moon is a master of metaphors, and even during the sparse breaks between episodes of ultra-violence, I never grew tired of what I tarnished (and fueled) my mind with. This novel only reaffirmed my destiny-driven desire to collaborate with this budding genius of bizarro horror.

And fortunately, I remembered our fallopian conversation. And despite the peril of never knowing whether or not he was, in fact, a deity, a lifelong friendship was unavoidable.

Within his most recent and evolved collection, Jonathan Moon conjures snippets of thoughts that a normal subconscious mind would dare to admit.

Cringe.

Shudder.

Smirk

... and laugh.

For humor of the blackest kind lurks within and breeds within dystopian realities. It's a marriage of spit and bib, and an original ride through a tarnished road of madness and broken smiles. There is still a lingering innocence that helps dictate these tales, but it's an innocence that casts a much more sinister grin. I consider myself quite lucky to have personally watched his writing grow steadily more jaded. This satanic Dennis the Menace traded in his slingshot and now packs a bazooka.

Jason "Wookie" Wuchenich

11:58 p.m. February 7th or August 13th, 2012

# HEART OF AN ANGEL

I have the heart of an angel.

I keep it in an old rusty birdcage on my table. There is a perch in the cage where the demon parakeet used to sit, but the angel heart doesn't take advantage of it. It just floats there glowing like the un-light from a dead star, keeping my old cabin an uncomfortable eerie warm.

The demon parakeet never did anything but howl and curse, froth and spit, and occasionally make all the meat in the cabin go rotten all at once. Sometimes I miss the hateful bastard. The angel heart convinced all the dogs to up and kill themselves all on the same damn day. Dead dog days take a lot out of a person. The day the dogs all died, the angel heart kept me up all night with a barking weeping fit. Tendrils, strands of pure light, reached from its pulsing surface through the cage at me. I burned their tips with my Zippo lighter. Heavenly heart fingers are no match for butane and flame.

During a fierce high-mountain windstorm, the angel heart tried to make me to do myself in. It hummed and

12

glowed all loving and creepy while it sprouted a white-hot beard of tendrils. The tiny tentacles danced before my tired eyes and convinced me I needed the sensation of brisk wind upon my face. My legs walked me through the old wooden door. I could vaguely hear it slamming itself as I walked away, as if it didn't want to be left alone with the angel heart. My legs walked me to the edge of the ridge, and the angel heart spoke to me with a voice like longsuffering coral and told me it was a nice day for a glide.

My toes dislodged rocks and pebbles, and they danced down the steep ridge face. I was very close to jumping, with mindnumbing faith, and falling to a terrible doom. Luckily for me, my eyes saw through the trance and took sight of the carving of a man and his dogs chasing down a legless dragon across the wide trunk of an old pine tree. The carving I was doing when I saw the angel crash to earth in a clutter of light, love, and feathers. I remember the day with uncharacteristic clarity. The demon parakeet smelled unconscious angel and talked one of the dogs into opening the cage, most likely by the threat of rotten meat. It took on its much less flattering natural form as it dove onto the angel broken on the rocks below. I tell you now; you haven't seen degradation until you've seen how a demon really fucks an angel.

I clutched the tree upon which I was carving. Splinters dug into the soft flesh of my cheeks and forehead, but I couldn't watch the terribly violent copulation at the bottom of the ridge. Finally, I heard the demon flap away, hellishly content. Perhaps he flew off to become a parakeet again, to howl and curse, froth and spit, and spoil someone else's meat. I looked around the tree, blood and sap smeared all over my face, and beheld the mutilated corpse below. The angel's chest was torn wide open, its devastated ribcage releasing that eerie glow through shards of splintered bone. I scurried down the ridge-side to see why the corpse was glowing and saw the angel heart blackening as the body died. I stabbed it with a stick and carried it home, held out a distance in front of me. I was planning on eating it, since all the meat had maggots swimming through it, but the angel heart purred when I set it in the demon parakeet's vacated cage. I watched it pulse and twitch until it began floating.

The dogs howled their disapproval, but I didn't want to touch the angel heart once it resurrected. It stayed in the cage and eventually talked those disapproving dogs to death. It won't get me. I warned it the day I buried my dogs. Its tendrils flicked love and understanding at me, but my own heart has grown cold, even in its cursed warm glow.

The angel heart will never understand that some of us don't want salvation; we just want our rotten meat back.

# REAL LOVE BURNS (STPYEOT Remix)

My girlfriend pulls slivers from under my fingernails.

After we fuck, I hold her hair back while she pukes.

We are Bonnie and Clyde. We are Mickey and Minnie. The Alpha and the Omega and the Meat in the middle.

Her name is January, though she has a March temper and an October smile. My name doesn't matter none.

Once, we fled to the forest for safety. We danced naked under the stars, then pointed up at them, finding the monsters hiding in the clouds. Then a black dog wandered into our makeshift camp. It looked at us with mismatched eyes, one sterling blue and the other a dark rainbow of neons. We stared it down with our bloodshot eyes, all red, dry, and bitter. It stank of shit and fire. We reeked of sweat and sex. A crowd of birds and demons gathered in the surrounding trees to watch our confrontation. Slow rain fell around us.

The black dog walked a slow, smelly circle around us while the demons and birds chattered amongst themselves. I gazed up at our sudden audience, but the black dog and January ignored them, since they were stalemating in a stink-eye contest.

The black dog stood upright on its hind feet and addressed us with a sneer, "You can't fuck here."

"It's wide-open forest," we told it in eerie unison. "We can fuck wherever we want."

My eyes darted back to the demons and birds. January kept staring down the black dog. The black dog saw us in one eye and the future in the other. That eye clouded over, blind. The slow rain stirred the dust from the forest floor in tiny explosions of filthy reason. The mud-drops shimmered images of past, present, and ever-hellish future as they exploded skyward, then hailed gravity's mercy and plopped back to the ground to repeat the process with smaller drops and thickening prophetic memories in dirt-crusted clarity. The black dog and January both ignored the raindrop vision quest and the chittering demons and birds above.

"They don't understand!" the     demons and    birds squawked at me.

"I hear you, God damn it!" I shouted and shook my fist as an added visual aide of my inner frustration at their stubborn ignorance. January and the black dog continued their stare-fight, and the demons and birds gazed down upon me with glowing orange eyes accentuating their scowls.

Suddenly, the black dog conceded to January's fierce hawk-eye glare and turned to me. He pointed his paw at me, and I watched blood drip slowly from the split pads.

"You," the black dog told me, "haven't hurt enough today."

The demons and birds screeched rowdy appreciation, and January finally noticed them. She screamed as they swooped down and attacked her. The rain pelted flapping wings and was flung away soiled as they tore her skin from her body in thin pink strips. The black dog doubled over with raspy laughter as they skinned my sweetheart with beaks and claws and teeth and talons. I felt my eyes turn purple and my knuckles turn white. I reached into the swirling mess of feather, flesh, and hideous demon hide. I couldn't reach sweet January before they finished their cruel task. They flapped back to their branches above with strips of her tender flesh dangling from their beaks and maws.

While I was watching the birds and demons make their satisfied retreat, January's voice ran screaming into the tangled darkness of the woods. It radiated panic back in waves of bright colors that left red and blue spots to dance in my vision. January cowered, humiliated at her total nakedness.

The black dog pointed and laughed at us. January couldn't look at me, and I couldn't see past her pulsing twitching muscles to her beautiful skinless face. Our guilt and love mingled like the mud-drop visions and left the same dirty feeling. She left me then, to find new skin.

After she withdrew, the clearing hummed, empty save for me and the black dog. He opened his mouth to say something, but, having decided I did not value his opinion, I smashed him in the head with a sharp heavy rock I found conveniently waiting at my bare feet. He fell to the ground, a skull fracture closer to death. He tried to stand on wobbly legs, but I rewarded his tenacity with a second and third crack across the skull. As soon as his death twitches ceased, I used my jagged murder tool to skin the black dog and then hung its fleshless carcass from a nearby tree. I wrapped myself in his bloody pelt to hide my shame and sorrow.

I wandered the forest, lost and dazed, in my new black dog suit. As I stumbled deeper, I lost my humanity with each crooked step. I crawled over decaying logs and slithered over stones slick with neon mosses of pink and green until I happened upon a gently rushing creek. The water was clear enough that I could easily see the rocks and knives below the surface. The stones were worn shiny-smooth and the blades worn deathly sharp by the incessant babbling of the ancient stream.

I knelt on the creek bed and tried to wash the black dog's blood from my hands. The blood warmed the creek water as it chipped away from the lines and cracks of my hands. Steam rose but hung close to the surface, hiding the slick stones and hungry blades below. Try as I might, I

19

couldn't help but slice my knuckles on the underwater knives. Patient clouds of red spirited away from me in a hurry to smooth stones and sharpen blades downstream.

I shivered and sweated there, drifting in the cold wet culling song of the creek. My heavy eyelids dipped, dipped, closed. Like a wheezy death rattle, I felt my soul slip out of my mouth and down my chin in a dribble of drool that splashed weakly into the cool mountain water. I felt my soul flipped and tickled by the current's erstwhile tumble and roll. It glided along slippery stones, then was dragged through a patch of swaying razor blades. It cut and tore; it burned and screamed. Blood first filled my vacant eyes, then drizzled down my bearded face.

January's sparkling voice peeked around a machete blade in the deepest part of the creek, where it chose to seek refuge. It bubbled up from its hiding spot, peeling my tattered soul from the blades as we rose toward the surface. A tiny orange frog snapped at my shredded soul, and January's voice responded by jerking its jaws wide open and stuffing my soul inside. It bloated awkwardly and kicked furiously away from January's ruthlessly sweet voice. The orange frog jumped out of the water and onto my leg. With great effort and much internal urging from my twisting kicking soul, the frog hopped up my slouched form, all the way into my slack-jawed mouth. I chewed and tasted frog. My soul slipped in like a whisper. I blinked blood out of my eyes to see beautiful January standing on the other side of the creek.

January's voice had found her body, and January had found new skin. Nice new skin with bright pretty tattoos and deep purple scars.

"Do you like my new skin?" she asked shyly, still feeling exposed beyond her naked flesh.

"I do! I love it, and I love you!" I blurted back.

I modeled my black dog suit.

"I love it! It cloaks your regret and melancholy so well! And it brings out your cold dead heart."

I blushed and felt cold chunks of gore against the hot flesh of my cheeks.

A familiar voice spoiled our lovers' reunion from above, "You can't wear that here!"

Together, we looked up. The skinned dog hung from the jaws of a bright yellow hunchbacked demon like an angry scrap of discarded innards.

"Okay," I answered calmly.

The demon smiled and opened his mouth, allowing the skinned dog to fall with a squishy splat. I took his coat from my shoulders and waved it tauntingly, like a matador. The demons and birds cheered. January cheered. The dog, all wet muscle and tissue, dove for his skin, but missed when I jerked it away and stepped around him. The demons and birds and girlfriend cheered louder. The dog growled ferociously, more determined by embarrassment, yet failed a second attempt. His skinless paws caught no traction, and he slid into the trunk of a wide tree The forest came alive with a nightmare of joyous cheers, an

21

aural energy so powerful it forced pinecones from the trees in its wake.

Strange sympathy rose within me, and I felt pity for the dog. I looked at January, and she looked at me. The forest fell silent. The stream still flowed, but the water sank closer to the rocks and knives to muffle the sound of itself. January smiled at me, a promise and demand and dare all present in her lovely grin. I handed the poor animal back his skin. A few demons and birds booed, but the words wrapped around the tree trunks and sank into the mud.

The skinned dog grabbed it without looking at me. I maintained a firm grip until he did. Once we made eye contact, I asked, "You know what this means?"

He nodded once, begrudgingly, and I let go of his skin. He climbed into his skin and twisted and wiggled until it felt comfortable again. The black dog looked at me and whined quietly.

"Is there any other way?"

I thought. January thought. Neither of us knew what the other was thinking, but I spoke for both of us. "I feel naked now, and she has already lost hers once today. Can you find us spare skins?"

"Impossible!" the black dog gasped. "We are too far away from town, and all the humans around are bone, dirt, and lies."   January and I both frowned.

"Too bad," we said in our eerie, adorable unison.

"Yeah." The black dog shrugged and burst into crackling green flames.

The host of demons and birds flapped from their branches in a panic. A booger-green demon yielded to a swirling pink fireball. A fat robin erupted into a toxic orange sunburst. The shadow-dark forest glowed with the exploding demon and bird fireworks. Carnage surrounded us, so dazzling and fleshconsuming. The neon flames licked the dry tree branches and engulfed the ancient forest quickly.

January and I held hands and swayed under the rainbow of fire as the black ash of trees and dreams floated around us.

I caught a handful of hot ash, and it burrowed under my fingernail. I watched her go to work digging the burning embers out. I could smell our anticipation in the smoke of the forest blaze and felt her heartbeat quicken like butterfly wings against my skin. We are in love, and real love burns.

# POISONED MEAT

Everything happened so fast.

Bobby blinks the blood out of his eyes and tries to catch his breath. He can't feel his legs, and for that, he is thankful. He lays his rifle across his lap and uses his hands to crawl to a tree behind him. Agony flares in his back as he drags his smashed legs away from the carnage of the clearing. His ears are ringing from all the sudden screams and close-range gunfire. The high buzzing sound makes understanding what just happened to him nearly impossible. His mind flashes back to this morning with more vivid clarity than that with which he perceives his gory current situation.

X

He woke with the sun, excited about his first day as a "hunter." Bobby splashed cold water on his face from the pan next to his bed and bounded from his tent into the dawn. He bent down and zipped his tent closed quickly before putting on his gloves. He was in a hurry, but he allowed himself a minute to soak in the beauty around the camp. He breathed the cold mountain air into his lungs, and he rushed off through the rows of tents to the makeshift garage.

Bobby was born and raised in the city, but the cities belonged to the dead now. The camp was called "Resurrection," and it was located high on a mountain ridge, far above the shambling dead. Tall evergreens surrounded the camp, and the 400 campers had built a few tall lookout/defense towers that rose even farther into the sky. Bobby loved the view from the towers and, unlike others who had tower-watch duty, he never complained. From the top, he could see down into the venison cages below or clear to the once-lush valley floor at the foot of their mountain. Others complained about the smell of deer shit and the freezing wind. He'd known that once he turned eighteen, he would be able-bodied enough to become a "hunter," and that day had finally arrived.

David was standing right outside the door to the garage, smoking a cigarette, when Bobby approached. The older man nodded and stepped to one side, allowing Bobby into the garage where the hunters gathered. David crumbled out his smoke and followed Bobby inside. Bobby walked into the room, and everyone turned to look at him. He stared back at the men and women he admired, and smiled nervously. Blake and Todd both nodded to him, and Shannon smiled, but no one said anything. Their eyes were all cold, and Bobby shivered slightly as they bored into him.

"Our new hunter," David growled at them, "Say hello."

A meek chorus of greetings and muttered introductions made Bobby blush, and David nodded at his flushed cheeks with a small grin. David strode to the wall and waited for everyone to surround him.

"This should be a nice easy run today, folks," he told them with the confidence of a born leader.

"We haven't had any sightings of black-bloods, human or beast, in at least three days," he told them over his shoulder while tapping on the map tacked to the wall.

"That doesn't make me excited," Buck grumbled. "It makes me nervous."

Buck was one of the largest men in the camp, and he was noticeably the biggest hunter. His size afforded him great attitude, and he often shared it. He had been a bully before the dead started rising, and that hadn't changed any when they ate everyone he ever knew. He had been one of the first to camp, and he had been a steadfast defender of the camp, but he really was an intolerable prick most of the time. David smiled at Buck as if he'd expected Buck to grumble.

"What are you smiling about?" Buck asked, anger twitching at his lips.

"I know why you're nervous, Big Man," David said, shaking his head slowly. "You're thinking that something is scaring everything else away, aren't ya?"

Surprise sparkled in Buck's eyes, and he nodded suspiciously at David.

"Noted. You, Blake, and Carol are on the four-wheelers. Load up the big guns if it makes you feel safer ..."

Buck interrupted him with a growl, "I'm not that worried about me, Little Man, I'm worried for the camp..."

David waved his hand and interrupted Buck back. "I didn't mean to hurt your feelings or make you feel challenged. Let me rephrase. I think you should load up the big guns; I'd sure feel safer."

Bobby swallowed hard as the mood in the cold room bristled with Buck's anger. David knew Buck to be a bully, but he wasn't afraid, as he'd dealt with bigger, badder men—dead and alive. David could fight the dead (or black-bloods as they were referred to in camp,) and he knew how to track them. Not that human black-bloods needed much tracking, but their undead animal counterparts still had their base instincts, and that was a very dangerous thing for the band of survivors.

Shannon spoke quickly, before anyone else could. "The camp would feel safer if we were out checkin' traps and laying new ones instead of sittin' in here primin' your testosterone to hunt dead things."

David and Buck exchanged looks, but any argument was stopped dead in its tracks. David broke the hunters into their four member teams, and the twelve living humans set out for the wall that surrounded the camp to face the death all around them.

X

The ringing in Bobby's ears has tuned down to a loud hum, and he can hear someone nearby gagging and taking deep ragged breaths. He pulls himself alongside the trunk of an ancient evergreen so he doesn't have to look at the small clearing and the crimson and black splattered and pooling there. He wipes blood off his face, but his hands are numb inside his gloves, and blood smears into his eyes. He winces while pulling off his gloves and dropping them next to his broken form. Every movement hurts. His hands are shaking and pale, but they wipe the blood from his eyes.

Bobby leans back against the tree trunk and tries to take deep breaths. He knows he has to calm down; there is no point in freaking out now. But every time he inhales, a sharp fiery pain flares up and down his left side. He chokes on his breath and spits a mouthful of bright red blood all over himself. With the blood comes a release of pressure in his chest, and he seizes the chance to lean forward. He looks from his broken and twisted legs, where each foot is pointed too far in an odd direction, to the bloody trail he left dragging himself to shelter. The small swath of pine needles and gore ends abruptly at the corpse of the half-rotted black-blood elk.

## X

Bobby checked the stock in his semi-auto rifle twice while the group waited for the wall to be raised. The only opening in the entire wall was one ten-foot-wide section where the wall would slide up through a system of jerry-rigged pulleys. The entrance was built near the bottom of a steep rock outcropping to prevent any wandering black-blood from finding the one weak spot in the tall log wall. Built high above and on either side of the gate were two guard planks, each occupied by one heavily armed man. Neither sentry looked down on the group as the gate rose slowly.

As soon as the gate allowed enough room, Buck roared his fourwheeler out and up the rocks. The two other four-wheelers, driven by Blake and Carol, followed. The remaining nine filed two by two out the opening and up the rocks on foot.

Bobby allowed everyone past until he was the last. A wide-smiling Todd settled in next to him. As they walked through the gate, Todd asked, "How long you been inside, Bobby?"

Bobby didn't look back at Todd; he just focused on the steep path cut up the wall. He barely remembered entering the camp. Even walking up the same path he'd walked down at some point couldn't bring back his blacked-out memories.

After a moment of going unanswered, Todd said, "That long, huh?"

Bobby flushed and turned to the ever-smiling man, "I'm sorry, sir. I don't remember much about before I got here."

Todd smiled, retrieved a floppy fisherman's hat from his vest, and pulled it over his shiny bald head. He chuckled, a warm, friendly sound that calmed Bobby's nervousness, and told Bobby, "First thing, easy with that 'sir' shit. Nobody out here likes to be called 'sir.' Well, maybe Buck, but he's an asshole." Todd chuckled again and then said, "Second, feel lucky you can block it out."

"Yeah," Bobby sighed. "I hear them at night. You know, people who remember."

Todd smiled his good-natured grin and nodded. They climbed the rest of the rocky path in silence. Once at the top, Bobby stood and stared out in near disbelief. The camp sat high atop a ridge, and the survivors had burned the valley around them to ash. The mountainside had been furiously logged for the wall but otherwise left untouched, as the hard terrain and thick trees offered seclusion and natural defense. As he stared out through the trees to the blackened valley below, memories flooded back to Bobby, and they overwhelmed him. He knelt on the ground, and tears warmed his eyes. Only Todd was standing close enough to notice, and he helped Bobby back to his feet before anyone else saw his momentary breakdown.

Bobby wiped his eyes and managed a small smile. "I *was* lucky."

"Yeah, well, now you can move on," Todd told him quietly enough that no one else heard.

David turned from the larger group to face Bobby and Todd. "Just my luck," he said to them, "I get the funny guy and the new guy."

Todd bowed and snickered. "Your lucky day, Dave. Our shit luck, but your lucky day."

"Hey, you can switch with Shannon and go hang out with Buck if ya want," David smirked back.

"Easy, asshole," Todd warned through his wide grin.

Bobby laughed out loud, and David's smile matched Todd's.

"You ever been hunting, Bobby?" David asked as they walked to Carol and her camouflaged four-wheeler.

"Once, when I was just a boy," Bobby answered honestly.

"I think a better question would be, "You killed a mess of dead things yet, Bobby?" Todd interjected with a grin.

"Good point, and I was working toward it," David answered before walking over to Carol.

Carol and David talked and pointed downhill while Bobby checked his stock for the fifth and sixth time. Todd just chuckled softly and shook his head at the nervous kid. Carol fired her ATV to life and drove in the direction she and David had been pointing. David nodded after her, and all three started walking down the hill.

"We're checking traps today, Bobby. As I said before, it should be easy, but with black-bloods, you never know. Our cages are strong, but they can't hold everything. Undead animals are fiercer and way more reckless than their living counterparts. Same rules apply: Shoot them in their fucking heads," David told Bobby.

Bobby nodded his understanding, and David continued, "Make no mistake, Bobby, we are hunters, and we are hunting.

We are hunting poisoned meat, and it fights back."

X

The black-blood elk is lying in a puddle of gore in the middle of the small clearing. Even though Bobby blew its decayed brains out of its rotted skull, it still looks to be staring him down with one hungry, dead eye. Half of its face and head are missing, and broken chunks of elk teeth are scattered around. One gray antler points to the sky with blood slowly dripping down it. Bobby clenches and unclenches his fists while he stares at the massive twice-dead beast. His body is growing cold from blood loss, and he stops clenching in favor of shaking.

To the left of the elk, Bobby can see what's left of David, and it almost makes him sick. He gags and then chokes. Pain flares from his side and chest as he turns back away from David. Bobby sees Carol next; she is broken and bent in a bloody heap. Her corpse is near the pines where her four-wheeler was tossed by the rampaging black-blood elk. On the other side of the elk, Bobby spots Todd gagging and choking on his own blood. He rolls weakly in the dirt with his hands pressed, tight but useless, to the massive wound on his neck. Bobby watches wordlessly as Todd's gags turn to gurgles and his hands flop away from his torn-out throat. Bobby sobs and looks behind the elk corpse at the destroyed cage covered in both fresh and black blood.

X

David and Todd led Bobby up and down the steep paths with the pace of men eager to either kill something or get the hell home. The hunters had placed traps ranging in size from small enough for rodents to large enough for bears. Dozens of traps were scattered across the forest floor, and Bobby got his first chance to catch his breath when they came upon a cage containing a yowling and hissing undead bobcat. Fury darkened its dead eyes as it saw them, and it crouched and drew its claws from skinless paws. David blew its brains out and trembled noticeably.

"Not good, fellas. Not good at all," David told them, all humor gone from his tone. "A predator like this could infect an ungodly number of smaller creatures. The smaller the black-blood creature is, the harder it is to stop spreading. Birds, easy prey for this fella, can fly over the

33

wall. An infected rodent will gnaw through our wall, and the camp will be chaos and death before we have any chance to stop it."

They used a long barbed hook Todd carried to pull the thing out of the trap before David dug into his pack and pulled out a small slab of fresh meat to re-bait it. As they started for their last stop, a small clearing with a big cage, David finished, "Black-bloods can still hunt. It is part of their instinct when they're hungry. They are always ravenous and vicious. I swear to God above, dead things are stronger than living things, animals and humans. That is what makes an undead natural predator so God damned dangerous."

He was going to say more, but just then, they entered the clearing. Both David and Todd raised their guns the instant they saw the mangled cage. David grabbed his walkie-talkie and made a frantic cry to Carol while Bobby raised his gun and stepped closer to David to allow him some cover.

"Let's hope to God that bobcat was in this cage first," Todd said in a vain attempt to ease the fear they all felt.

"Yeah, I don't think so," David said while scanning the tree line through his scope, "I don't know what happened, but there is fresh blood and black blood. We could be looking at two of them."

They sat in nervous silence, guns at the ready, until the roar of the ATV cut through the surrounding forest.

Carol pulled into the clearing and turned off the ATV. She looked at the men and then at the smashed cage. The sweet smell of decay reeked around them, and the air seemed to stir. She looked nervously at them, and as she reached for her gun, the black-blood elk thundered out of the tree line and charged her.

X

Bobby can hear the sound of people and ATVs approaching. He has lost so much blood he can hardly sit up. His torso feels heavy, and it tries to pull him to the ground. He almost lets it, but then Todd twitches. Bobby gasps and strains to stay sitting up. Todd's fingers curl and uncurl. Bobby grabs his gun, but drops it when it seems hundreds of pounds heavier than it did before. He grunts and pulls it onto his lap.

Todd's eyes blink, and he starts to roll back and forth, spilling blood out of his wounds.

Bobby checks his clip, finds it empty, and begins searching his pockets for a new one.

Todd rolls awkwardly into a sitting position, and he stares at Bobby with black eyes, black blood flowing from his throat.

Bobby attempts to slam the clip into the gun, but he doesn't have the strength to make it lock.

Todd snarls and stumbles to his feet, never taking his eyes off of Bobby.

35

Bobby strains and tries to slam the clip home, but fails.

Todd takes a few slow steps forward as if relearning how to walk.

Bobby screams in pain and frustration as he slams the clip one last time. It clicks loudly into place.

Todd growls and stumbles for Bobby.

Bobby raises his rifle, but is distracted by a shadow moving in the trees behind Todd.

Todd slaps the rifle away from Bobby and falls on him. He howls, and blood splatters Bobby's face. At the moment Todd snaps forward, his head explodes with the crack of highpowered rifle fire. His body falls next to Bobby's. Bobby's ears are ringing again. Buck and all the others rush into the small carnagefilled clearing. Blake stands over Carol's now-twitching corpse and fires a round into her skull. Buck walks over to Bobby and points his rifle at Bobby's forehead.

Bobby pushes the barrel away weakly and tries to talk, but blood is bubbling in his throat. He wants to warn them. Buck kicks his arm away from the gun and points the gun back at Bobby's head. Bobby rolls to the side so he doesn't have to see it coming. In the split second before the bullet slams through his head, he sees the black-blood cougar crouched in the tree line behind Buck.

# ROADSIDE CROSSES

*Mile Marker 174*

Her sobs make him angrier. Never at him, in the way a man might feel guilt for letting his monster-side show and then aiming that feeling right back at whoever saw it. There is no guilt behind Wade Bocheque's verbally murderous rants at his mentally hobbled and feeble wife Susan. He means every word of every threat and, more often than not, backs them up in his brutal way.

Insecurity warps into jealously warps into paranoia warps into rage.

His fury makes his face hot. Despite the blistering winter winds rocking his old LeBaron, his window is down. Beads of sweat drip through his thick black eyebrows and off his cavemanlike brow. He grips his steering wheel so hard his knuckles pop; years of breaking them over Susan's head have taken their toll on the cartilage. He uses the grinding sensation as bone rubs against bone to push himself over the edge. He grabs his cell phone off the passenger seat and steps on the gas. The wheels spin on the icy road before the worn tires find any traction. The rear end fishtails in response, but Wade's foot remains on the pedal, and luck straightens out the vehicle. He dials while cursing the windshield wipers for icing up.

The highway turns as it slopes up through a pass. Traffic slows to forty miles an hour as the wind whips through the fields, kicking up snow in the form of a furious drifting monster thrashing up the mountainside. Wade squints through his icestreaked windshield and swerves into the oncoming lane to see around the semi in front of him. Headlights stab through the swirling snow, and Wade cranks the LeBaron back behind the semi. He taps his fingers on the torn leather steering wheel while the phone rings. She doesn't answer by the second ring, so he assumes she is fucking someone. He is running down the mental list of men she could be getting fucked by when she answers on the fourth ring.

"Wade, oh my God, where are you?"

Wade scoffs under his breath. "You wanna know if you got time to get your fucking boyfriends outta the house before I get back?"

"Wha-wha-what? No. No, they just said on the radio that they are closing the highway. I just wanted to make sure you're all right."

Wade doesn't hear her words. He hears the fear in her voice, and his dick gets hard. He plans on yelling at her every mile of the way, breaking her down into a weeping shell of a woman and building himself into a sexual rage frenzy satisfied only by her gagging sobs and the feel of slick blood sticking their naked bodies together.

"You lying slut bitch!" he screams over the howling wind.

"No, Wade …"

"Shut the fuck up, you stupid whore. I can't die; someone has to keep an eye on a slut like you. If you didn't have me, you would have fucked half the town by now. You would tear apart families, offerin' married men yer chewed-up snatch. Admit it, you whore!"

His prick pushes against his jeans, and his thick lips curl up in a malicious smile. She will scream apologies now. She will beg. And he will show no mercy. He swerves over for another look around the semi. Headlights flood his iced and cloudy windshield. Wade curses into the phone as he swerves back, barely missing the pickup the blinding lights adorn. The passing truck flings frozen slush across Wade's already obstructed windshield.

Wade breathes a few husky breaths into the phone and yells, "You got nothin' to say now, bitch?"

He hears her take a deep, shaky breath.

"Fuck you, Wade. I'm done."

She isn't crying. She isn't breaking. This isn't working.

Confidence warps into frustration warps into rage.

"Fuck you, Susan; you will never be done with me. You stupid twat."

"No, Wade, I'm leaving. I've got my bags packed, and I've got an appointment with a lawyer in the morning."

Wade's anger rises so suddenly he can't form words to express it. He just growls curses as he swerves around the semi, this time without looking. Headlights in the near distance, distorted by the whipping snow, blind him, but his fury makes his foot heavy. He swerves back into his own lane, cutting off the semi and earning a horn and bird combo from the driver, and narrowly avoiding the oncoming car, which also honks at his lackluster driving skills. He returns the bird as the LeBaron slides back and forth across the black-ice-covered highway.

"We'll see about that, you confused bitch."

"No, Wade, we won't. I mean it; I'm done."

Her voice is stronger than it's been in years. He thought he'd completely broken her, made her unable to stand on her own against him. Her nerve infuriates him. Wade navigates the uphill highway through a tiny slot of unclouded glass. He manages the first of two perilous turns at the top of the pass.

"Fuck you! You aren't leaving me! No one leaves me! Do you understand me?"

The rear wheels of the LeBaron lose traction first. The back end spins toward the side of the road, sending fans of freezing slush into the steel safety railing. The front wheels lock up, and the entire car spins out of control. The brakes scream as Wade slams on them, but the car's momentum carries it toward a separation in the guard rail at breakneck speed.

"This is over when I say it is over. And it ain't fucking over! Do you hear me, Susan? You stupid bitch!"

The LeBaron slams into the safety railing while Wade berates her. The rail is made of a line of steel hammered to stout wooden posts, and when the car connects with it, the steel pops off the posts and shears through the rear passenger-side door. The glass from the passenger-side windows shatters inward, slicing strips of flesh from his face. The steel rail tears through Wade's seat, and he throws himself into the steering wheel in a frantic effort to avoid its jagged edge. The car comes to a complete stop with the rail just barely digging into his back. He can feel his shredded flannel shirt flapping against his sides and blood running in torrents down his back into a pool at his ass crack.

The windshield shatters upon impact, and the wind bites at Wade's exposed and bleeding face. The snow is whipping to the point where he can barely see the end of the demolished safety rail. The car has come to rest in such a way that only the very end of it is sticking out into the highway. Wade chuckles at his good luck, and blood gurgles up his throat. He coughs, which sets his lungs on fire, and spits dark red blood out the empty space formerly occupied by the windshield. Most gets blown back in his face.

He hears Susan screaming and realizes slowly that he still has a death grip on his cell phone. She heard the whole thing. The squealing brakes. The twisting metal. The shattering glass. She might have heard him scream.

He pulls the phone close and snarls at her, "Call me an ambulance, you fucking whore. The fucking road is covered in black ice, and this piece of shit car got impaled on a fucking safety rail."

She says nothing. Her breathing is slower, not as confident.

"God damn it! Call me a fucking ambulance, you-"

The headlights from the semi splash across Wade's pale bloody face in the same instant that the driver sees the wreckage. The big truck wiggles and threatens to spin out, but the driver thinks quickly and drops a gear as he gets a handle on the road. As it whips back into line, the rear end slides just far enough over to tap the front end of Wade's car.

The air bag goes off, forcing the jagged steel rail through Wade's spine, then his sternum as he is slammed back. His fingers clench tight enough to crush his cell phone, ending the call with Susan still sobbing softly on the other end. His spinal cord is severed, and his head flops forward onto his chest. As Wade dies, he coughs up shards of bone and shits himself.

The LeBaron is torn open from the crash, and Wade's blood runs from his many wounds and drips off the car to the frozen ground below. All the evil and insanity, all the violence and predatory impulse, all the jealousy and insecurity drips out of him. A thick black sludge, the essence of the man too foul to enter Heaven's gate follows the path of the blood as it drips, and it steams when it joins the growing puddle on the side of the road.

### Mile Marker 177

Susan Bocheque hurts differently than she expected. Standing on the side of the road in the spot where Wade died, she expected old feelings to rumble. In the days following his death, the snow turned to rain. The ice on which the LeBaron slid has melted away, leaving shards of metal and plastic to glisten across the road even during the gray day. She stares at the black-and-red stain soaked into the ground and can only muster more anger. Anger at the years she spent under Wade's thumb. His rapehappy ways and punching-bag tendencies overshadowed any joy they ever found together.

A toxicology report showed that Wade was on high on meth when he crashed, voiding his life insurance policy. Susan was left nothing but an escape. She stands on the side of the road now, a plain white wooden cross in her shaking hands as she talks to the Wade stain.

"I told you I was leaving, Wade. I'm going to be safe now. I'm going to find the happiness you told me I didn't deserve."

Susan takes a few stuttered breaths at the release of the words. She blinks a few times as fog rolls up from over the stilldestroyed safety rail. Her eyes are wet, but she channels years of memories to keep the tears at bay. She is a new woman, and she will give him no more tears. She reminds herself and dries her angry eyes on her sleeve.

"I want you to know," she starts, but repressed fury chokes her until a car speeds by, splashing a wave of road water inches from her feet as it passes. "I never cheated on you. You made me hate sex. You made me hate me. You made me afraid of love."

A few cars pass from both directions, and the moisture they stir as they pass makes the fog denser. She allows herself a few more breaths. She clutches the cross close to her chest, and splinters dig into her palm from the weak wood.

"But your good buddies Harry and Carl both hit on me. At *your funeral,* in fact."

Angry tears threaten to spill again, and she takes the breaths necessary to calm down. She is leaving him behind forever. He gets the cross, nothing more of her time or thought. It will be the one thing left of Wade Bocheque. All of his worldly possessions tainted with his dark aura are landfill bound. He was by no means a godly man in life, but Susan will mark his demise with a simple symbol with which he empathized little as a sign of her eternal indifference. She is proud of her choice, of her new mindset.

She considers the stain and wonders to herself if the ground has thawed enough for it. She will try once. If it breaks, she will toss it by the roadside and drive on to her new life without a second thought. Wade doesn't deserve anything more. With a grunt, she slams the cross down in the middle of the stain. It sinks into the gravel-littered roadside with ease. Susan wipes wood splinters off her palms by rubbing them together. The tiny white flecks speckle the dark stain below.

"Goodbye, Wade," she says out loud before turning away. Once she is facing away from the cross, the day seems brighter, and the fog between her and her car lifts lazily as she walks to it.

Behind her, the ground at the base of the cross bubbles, and a thick black slime oozes from it. Steam rises, and the stain boils. Her resolve makes him furious.

## Mile Marker 180

Lloyd shifts into fifth gear as the road begins its incline. He chuckles to himself at how smoothly his uncle's Corvette handles the twisting mountain roads. The bright neon-blue machine sticks out against the forest landscape as it passes other cars like it was shot out of a gun. Lloyd grabs the remote to the XM radio from the console and scans it to the punk rock station.

Bad Religion starts yelling about early man walking away and modern man taking control. Then Lloyd catches sight of someone sitting in the passenger seat. He turns slowly and takes in the man's grisly appearance. His head appears too heavy for his neck, and it hangs forward so the eyes glare up at him from under a small forehead bordered by bushy dark eyebrows. Below a squat, wide nose, two fat and bloody lips curl down in a frown. The man's chest is split wide open, ribs and sternum holding the skin taut on their jagged ends.

"Take me to Susan!" the specter screams in a voice like a blizzard.

Lloyd can't take his eyes off the mangled man, and the 'Vette begins to drift into the oncoming lane. He blinks rapidly, but the ghoul not only remains, he becomes violently irritated.

"You're as useless as she is!"

Lloyd doesn't even see the big white van bringing the local youth group home from an overnight camping trip. He stammers at the monster. The specter responds by reaching over and clawing at Lloyd's eyes. The driver of the van leans on his horn but doesn't swerve in time. The van plows through the Corvette's front end, and Lloyd snaps forward, shattering both legs and meeting the windshield of the van with his face. The force of the collision throws the conjoined vehicles through the steel guardrail. They land in a flaming heap, and smoke drifts up past the lone roadside cross.

## Mile Marker 179

Davy curses his luck at the weather. His big rig whines and shakes as he navigates the icy road. He has only been working for Kambitch Brothers Logging for two months, and hauling his loads past all the highway crosses always makes him nervous. The truck slows due to the slick incline, and he flicks on his hazard lights. Two pickups and a car speed past him and disappear in the blowing snow.

As he reaches the top of the pass, Davy notices a wide, stretched human face on the hillside. At first he thinks his mind is playing tricks on him, but the face in the snow turns its blind eyes toward him. Davy can't take his eyes off the face even as his rig starts to slide toward the safety rail.

The face contorts into a scowl and opens its mouth. Davy sees never-ending darkness inside for the split second before a massive white tongue rolls out of the mouth and lies, fat and wide, across the road. Davy tugs on his engine brake but moves too slow. The big truck hits the eight-foot-tall snowdrift and tips over. The massive logs on the trailer snap their bonds and roll in several different directions, smashing everything in their way. Sparks shoot from under the truck's cab as it slides toward the guard rail. The glass from Davy's window shatters, and he loses his grip. He falls to the concrete and is torn to shreds before he has time to scream.

The face on the hillside curls its lips into a smile as its snow tongue is blown away by the whipping winter winds. Redand-blue lights flash across the hillside face as a highway patrolman arrives on the scene. The wind howls, and the face slowly sinks back into the snow, leaving only a feeling of malevolence behind.

### Mile Marker 175

Officer Clinton Jocelyn pulls his highway patrol cruiser over between two dirty roadside crosses and puts it in park. He's been driving up and down the highway for the past six hours, and it's time to sit stationary and catch some speeders. He kills his headlights and flicks on his parking lights. Officer Jocelyn aims the radar at a distant set of headlights.

Out of the corner of his eye, he sees a squat man in his passenger seat. As he turns to face him, the man, with a gaping gory hole in his chest, lunges for the standard-issue shotgun all highway patrol carry. Clinton drops the radar gun between his knees and grabs at the shotgun as well. With a snarl, the dead man slams the butt of the shotgun into Officer Jocelyn's nose, shattering it and taking the fight out of the cop. The mangled man pokes the barrel under the cop's chin and pushes his head against the window.

"If you woulda' been there, that bitch couldn't have left me!"

48

The ghost gives Clinton no time to answer before pulling the trigger and blowing the cop's brains out of his car window. Pulpy matter mixes with shards of glass and splatters halfway across the highway. The headlights of oncoming cars shimmer and glow on the broken pieces of glass like gravel-bound stars.

### Mile Marker 176

Mildred gives her husband, Harold, a little poke in the ribs as they approach the incline of the highway. He gently swats her poking finger away and tells her, "Damn it. Don't go poking me."

"Do you see all these crosses?" Mildred holds her hand to her mouth and mumbles a prayer.

Harold considers the row of roadside crosses and shrugs. The road doesn't seem dangerous enough to have earned such a macabre audience, but the crosses start before they reach the top of the pass and then disappear with the turning road ahead. In his sixty-some-odd years Harold has never seen so many memorials. It chills him momentarily, but a black Honda Accord speeding toward him in the rearview grabs his attention.

"Well," Harold says nodding to his rear view mirror, "There might not be so many crosses if people didn't drive like this maniac."

"Oh, my." Mildred worries aloud as she turns to face the quickly approaching Honda.

As the Honda pulls even to pass a man glares from the passenger seat at Harold. The man's bushy dark eyebrows twitch when his thick lips curl down in a frown. The man reaches over and grabs the Honda's steering wheel. The driver shrieks and slaps at the man, who flings blood onto the windows with every jerking movement, but he pulls the speeding Honda into Harold and Mildred's old Cadillac.

A ball of flame erupts from under the Honda's hood and quickly engulfs the small black car as it spins out. The force of the collision launches the Cadillac into the trees standing guard over the mountain pass. Harold reaches over and grabs Mildred's hand as they flip into the trunk of a two hundred year old pine. The car crumbles against the thick base of the tree and pine needles flitter down and cover the smoking mess of metal.


### Mile Marker 178

Annabelle slows her Jeep Wrangler as she passes the small groups of crosses dotting the side of the highway. Her friends back at her dorm told her this was the most haunted stretch of highway in America but she didn't believe them until she sees the seemingly never ending string of crosses and flower arrangements dotting the roadside. The hair on the back of her neck stands on end. Then a man reaches from the back seat and wraps his filthy bloody hand in her hair. He pulls her backwards, twisting her neck painfully, and glares at her. His dark eyes squint under his bushy eye brows.

He yells, "Susan?" at her splattering blood and black slime across her face. She slams on the brakes and cranks the wheel hard to the left. The open top Jeep rolls six times before bursting into flames in the middle of the highway.

## Mile Marker 177

The snow is falling again. It whips and coats the thin layer of black ice that has covered the expanse of the pass. It blows up from the wide open fields and down from the towering pines.

A drift has half buried the cross left to mark Wade Bocheque; now faded and stained black from decades of road grime and weather. As the wind forces the snow around the drift at the base of the cross contorts and shapes into a swollen and stretched mask of Wade. The snow face rolls its blind eyes back and forth under bushy snow eye brows. The spirit can't see through the snow eyes or all it would see is a ten mile stretch of mountain highway littered with plain white crosses. He sniffs the air and smells a hitchhiker working their way through the storm towards him. The snow face sniffs again. It's not

Susan walking through the blizzard, just some other damned unlucky fool.

His relentless spirit has no sense of time so there is no way for him to know it has been forty years since she walked away. He only knows she hasn't passed by yet. There is no way for the wretched soul of Wade Bocheque to know that Susan lived a full life and died peacefully in her sleep. There is no way for him to know she had found enough love in the second half of her life with a kind caring woman that she really never gave him a thought after staking his cross into the road side. He only knows she hasn't passed by and he'll keep killing people until she does.

Her freedom makes him rancorous.

# CONVERSING DOCTOR DeFEO

Karen hears noises around her before she opens her eyes. She hears feet shuffle across a dirty floor, and she hears excited breathing only a few feet away. She opens her eyes, and daylight blinds her. She winces away from the light, and pain screams at the back of her head. She is standing against a chain-link fence, but she isn't outside. Karen tries to turn her head, and the pain flashes as her hair pulls from every direction. Her eyes are blurry from the agony in her head, and her legs feel weak and tired. Out of the corner of her teary eyes, she sees her hair, long and blond, tied to the fence behind her in dozens of sloppy knots. Her hands are held to her side by two ancient pairs of handcuffs. Her feet are free but useless with her hair tied so tight. She whimpers, and her eyes scan her makeshift prison.

The walls around her are made from old red brick. To the right the walls are ashen white as if a fire raged against them, stealing the bright red hue. Every ten feet or so, columns made from the same red brick are built from the dirty concrete floor to the drooping ceiling above, with tall metal shelves set in between. Old metal pipes and worn and exposed wires snake along the ceiling, disappearing above into the darkness around her. White ballasts for fluorescent lights hang along the ceiling, some dangling by only one end or the other, and the bulbs themselves are shattered and litter the floor, reflecting light weakly against the dark metal shelves. The bright rays of what she guesses is *morning* sunlight shine on her from a wide, dirty window shadowed like it is in a small adjoining room straight ahead of her. The shadows of the large brick room crowd the incoming sunlight into one thick ray that seems to smoke with the dust in the air. The light silhouettes the objects tossed on the metal shelves, casting horrible and distorted shadows that all seem to reach for her. Karen hears a sound that she can't identify, and she feels her skin goosebump all over.

Out of the corner of her eye, she sees movement on the other side of the shelf to her left. She tries to turn her head, but the knots hold her tight in place with a stubborn throb. A moan escapes her lips before she can stop it. The noise stops, and the silence makes the shadows seem denser. She wants to scream, but she knows it would be a waste of time and energy.

The shape on the other side of the shelf shifts, and Karen makes out the outline of a broad-shouldered man. She can't tell if he is wearing all black or if the darkness of the shadows cloaks him. The shape moves again and the creaking of an old chair echoes off the brick walls.

"Good morning," the shape says in a deep voice that sounds both wet and muffled. Something in the tone suggests that condescension is common for the speaker.

Tears well in Karen's eyes, and she clenches them closed, but the tears leak out the sides anyway.

"I said, 'Good morning,' Karen," the voice responds to her silence with the tiniest tint of malice. "Politeness dictates a timely reply."

Karen swallows hard and nearly chokes. Her throat feels like someone has strangled her to death's doorstep. Her tears slide down her cheeks, and they feel hot and uncomfortable. She has hundreds of questions but only asks, "Where am I?" in a dry, painful croak.

"You, Miss Myers, are in the basement of the building you were skulking around at three o' clock this morning," the voice answers flatly. The chair squeaks, and the man stands up and stretches his arms. His body creaks and pops loudly, as if he had been sitting perfectly still for hours.

Karen remembers the night in quick bursts of memory.

She remembers Jay—*dear God, where's Jay?*—picking her up from work and not even arguing with her when she insisted on visiting the abandoned asylum she had been studying about while researching Dr. Benjamin Clyde DeFeo, a once-genius doctor turned deranged killer.

Jay, playing the role of supporting boyfriend to excess, called and left a message on his boss's phone informing him that he was ill and would have to miss the day. The moon hung fat and spotted in the sky by the time the stumbled from the tree line and onto the grounds of the Medford Hospital for the Criminally Insane.

She remembers the chill that went through her blood when she walked the same path DeFeo walked while perfecting his torturous murder techniques on inmates at the former hospital for the criminally insane. Karen made Jay walk the burnt shell of Dr. DeFeo's former dwelling, which was scorched to the ground by vandals two decades before, and he hid his growing anxiety at the eerie and abandoned hospital grounds and her macabre tales of the doctor and his morbid deeds. The main building, where the madman was rumored to have spent most of his blood-soaked time, looked like most of the other buildings (long, square red-brick buildings consisting of at least two and no more than four stories), but it oozed a feeling of malevolence into the darkness surrounding it.

She remembers the two asshole cops stepping out of the shadows of the old administration building as Jay and she walked past in the moonlight. She remembers being rushed to the back of the administration building and shoved under the dirty white wooden porch. She remembers a whispered interrogation at gunpoint. She doesn't remember either of their names, but she knows they were looking for a killer they had somehow followed to the abandoned grounds. They told her and Jay to leave, and they were going to, but something stopped them— something large and gray and smelling of death. She remembers a big bony fist flying at her face and then blackness.

The rush of memories raises more questions but reminds her why her body feels smashed and beaten. The thought of her sweet Jay breaks her heart, and she knows he wouldn't have let anybody do this do her without a fight, a fight he must have lost. She can't hold the tears back any longer, and she begins to sob loudly. Each time her chest heaves, a painful lump throbs in her throat, and it hurts enough to make her cry even harder.

"Why?" she cries quietly to the stranger in the dark.

"Obviously, Miss Myers, you have never been fortunate enough to be schooled in the art of polite conversation," speaks the voice, loud enough now for Karen to tell it is a muffled baritone. "Typically, it is discourteous to answer a declaration with a question."

A floodgate of emotion has opened for Karen, and she can't form a reply around her sobs. Whines, chokes, and whimpers escape her, and when she does form a word, it is a halfwhispered "Please."

"Since, apparently, you are not in the mood to converse, I will take my leave." The chair in which the man has been sitting flies across the room with a clatter as if to punctuate the statement, bouncing through the dusty ray of sunlight and landing in the shadows. "I'll be back in a week to see if you feel like attempting a subsequent dialogue."

The man walks away from her, and Karen panics at the thought of being left alone for a week to starve and stand in the shadows alone. The panic grips her, and she shouts after the man even though it makes her throat feel like she is swallowing hot coals.

"Wait! Wait!" she sobs.

He doesn't respond, but she can still hear his shuffling feet.

"I'm sorry!" she moans. "Wait! I'm so sorry!"

The sound of his shuffling stops. She can hear him taking deep, ragged breaths to her right.

The muffled voice asks, "Beg your pardon?" in an irritated tone.

Karen flushes with relief, and she doesn't even know why. He has answered her pleas, and that fact gives her a false rush of hope.

Hope to reason with this madman.

Hope to survive.

"I'm sorry I was so rude." She tells him what her racing mind tells her he wants to hear. "I'd really like to talk ... uh ... converse."

"I cannot promise that I have the reserves of fortitude to deal with any further outbursts of such appalling conversational etiquette," the man says as he shuffles toward her.

"I understand, and I'm very sorry. I ..." Karen says and is interrupted by the man as he walks past her on the other side of the shelves.

"I don't believe I could even assure my ability to stay my hand, so true and steady, and keep it from flying to your face, carving out your tongue, and feeding it to my guardian while you watch." The man turns and looks at her as he passes through the ray of sunlight, but his six-foot frame blots out enough of the light to send Karen's world into total darkness, and she sees nothing. The darkness feels cold and invasive, and Karen whimpers. The man stands in place for a moment and lets Karen squirm before taking a slow shuffling step into the shadows to Karen's left.

"Is that a touch of merinthophobia there, Miss Myers?" the man asks as he bends with a loud, leathery creak and picks up the chair.

Karen searches her memory for boring Psych 114 lectures on phobias, as she could be displaying any number of phobias, considering she *is* tied to a chain-link fence in the darkened basement of an abandoned hospital for the criminally insane with an obviously unhinged sociopathic madman.

She doesn't dare to take too long with an answer and blurts the first thing that comes to her mind, "Yes, ever since I was a kid."

The man nods and places the chair next to the ray of sunlight and sits in it so a sliver of light falls on him. He is sitting facing Karen, and she can tell he is wearing a white mask of some sort, which covers his entire face. He folds his arms and sighs.

"And here I was jumping to the conclusion—a fair and easy error to make—that your mother was an uneducated whore and your father merely her swiftest and fiercest relative as your previous conversational etiquette indicated." He stops for a moment to watch Karen flinch at the words. "But if the incestuous pair punished you by tying you and binding you up tight, then at least they did something accurate. You should be scared right now, Karen. Any *living* person would be scared to be standing with your view and condition."

Karen sobs and tells him, "I was mistaken. I thought you meant fear of the dark."

"Not very bright are you, Miss Myers?"

"I guess not," she cries, and she hates herself for the whine she hears in her voice.

"Oh, now don't go feeling picked on," the voice says with a deep chuckle. "I feel that in your dire idiocy, you have mistaken my insult. I wasn't calling you brainless because you didn't know what fear merinthophobia represents to the low-browed layman. I was implying that you're insane for thinking you could lie to me about such."

"I don't know what to say," Karen whispers, "and I don't want to make you mad."

The man laughs, a hateful mocking sound, and claps his gloved hands. "That's better. Doesn't it feel so?"

Karen doesn't understand the question enough to even fake an answer, and she whimpers again in pained panic. The man mercifully takes her whimpers for an answer and continues. "I was referring to your honesty. But now I have decided that any attempt at civilized conversation I should dare will only end in my frustration. Shameful really, so let's try a new tactic."

The man stands and steps closer to Karen, the light illuminating the right side of him. He wears a thick black trench coat lined in ragged brown-and-tan fur. The mask he wears looks like a simple white porcelain face with dark brown smears added to emphasize tired bloodshot eyes, a wide comical nose, and a downturned mouth. Long black hair hangs in wisps over the mask and is visible on his wide shoulders.

He stops only a few feet away from her and speaks again in his muffled baritone. "We will forego conversation in favor of interrogation."

Karen's mind reels at the statement, thinking of the madman's potential interrogation techniques. If he expected polite conversation with people bound by their hair to chain-link fences tucked away in basements, what would he do to make his captives talk? As if he reads her mind, he raises his right hand slowly and deliberately through the sunlight, letting it gleam off the blade of the straight razor he is holding.

"I want to know why you were snooping about, at such an early hour, no less," he asks and tilts his head, awaiting her reply.

"I work for a newspaper," she begins, but he groans and interrupts.

"I know where you work, Karen. The police officers had it written down in their diminutive notebook. If I require backstory I will inform you of such."

He waits patiently for her to control her sobs and stumble for a response. She closes her eyes, unable to focus with the drawn, tired eyes of the mask staring at her and the gleaming razor in his hand. She keeps her eyes shut tight as tears leak down her cheeks, and she tells him, "I thought it was abandoned."

He nods. "It is abandoned. These walls," he holds his arms out to the red brick shadowed around them, "have been hailed as cursed by the living and left to decay and crumble in rumor and neglect. What, then, do you know of its abandonment?"

Karen had studied Doctor DeFeo since college, her research culminating in a thesis paper on the serial-killing doctor, and she knew boundless facts about the man and the hospital where he stalked his deranged victims. Yet, when he puts her on the spot, her mind goes blank. She

62

manages to stifle a whimper and strains to rein in her panic so she can answer before he uses the razor he wields so proudly.

"I know it has been closed for almost two decades." She waits a second, and when he remains silent, she continues. "They closed the doors permanently after the second riot in its hundredyear history."

"A riot? Really? What do you know of that?" the man asks, again tilting his head slightly.

"I know that one man was involved with both riots. That's all I know." She shivers in the silence while he stares at her through the tiny slits in the mask.

"What man?" he asks after an agonizing minute of utter silence.

Without thinking, she sobs the name, his name. "Doctor Benjamin DeFeo."

"What do you know of this DeFeo?"

"I've studied him since college, wrote my thesis on him."

He takes a few shuffling steps closer, and the sunlight reveals his entire mask except his left eye. She sees a bright blue eye staring at her through the slit in the mask.

"Are you mocking me?" he asks, his voice shaking with malice.

The tone, more than the words, scares her suddenly and intensely enough that she loses control of her bladder and pisses herself. She is confused, and the panic sounds whiny in her voice,

"What? … NO … I … no …"

"I am he."

She looks at the masked man but can't believe him. Doctor DeFeo had been in his house when it was set ablaze, and his remains were buried under an oft-desecrated tombstone in a cemetery mere miles away. She had seen the tombstone. Hell, she and her college friends once drank beers against it while telling embellished versions of the doctor's reputed atrocities.

"I repeat it for you now: I AM Doctor Benjamin Clyde DeFeo. I was born in 1913 to Ronald and Eloise DeFeo of Boston.
Twenty-two years later, I obtained a job as an assistant to Head Doctor Rodger Gambrel, in this very building."

Scared and caught off guard by the madman's claims, Karen begins praying in lieu of answering.

"If you think having your hair braided to a fence by my behemoth is torture, be glad you weren't a murderous crazy back in Dr Gambrel's time." He steps within inches of her, and Karen recoils the fraction of an inch she is able to. "The good Doctor Gambrel would tap a jagged-toothed steel wheel the size of a midsummer acorn," he holds his fingers in a circle to demonstrate the size, "into the side of your pretty little cranium." He taps the left side of her head hard enough to pull her knotted hair. "As his implement of sanity drilled through your skull, you would stop screaming. If you retained any control of your vocal cords—and, trust me, most didn't—you would manage only blubbering and babble. Then, for good measure, he would tap here." He taps the other side of her head, causing her to wince in agony. "By now, the old boy would be whistling any old melody that he had heard of late. He would whistle, and you would drool and moan, a morbid tune I've heard more times than you can imagine. The two of you would make your damned music, ignoring me and even each other while your souls brushed together like mating cosmic beings."

The man takes a deep, satisfied breath. "Taking away life is the greatest gift you can give someone."

He tilts his head as if awaiting agreement, but she digs deep and looks him in the one blue eye she can see. "I disagree."

He leans away and laughs the same angry sing-song laugh as before. "With what, Miss Myers? My sudden claim to my own, apparently famous, identity? Or has something else I have spoken been deemed disagreeable to you?"

Karen takes a deep breath, unsure how to continue. She fights the urge to crumble and cry, and she tells the man, "The Doctor DeFeo I studied believed he was dead for years before he was thought to have died. He went from being a doctor to a patient, and was believed to have perished during the second riot. I think he suffered ..."

65

"Oh, *I* have suffered. To set your poor befuddled history straight, *I* died during the *first* riot." As he finishes speaking, he reaches behind his head and loosens his mask. He reaches one gloved hand up and pulls the mask down slowly. "And, I assure you, *I* am dead now."

The man's face is twisted and scarred, mutated and shaped by burns and savage carvings. Patches of flesh across his face are different shades of color. His neck and chin are a sickly deep purple like a dog's underbelly, with a patchy black beard sprouting out of the diseased-looking skin. His bottom lip is swollen and spilt, while he is missing his upper lip, as well as his nose. Where his upper lip should be is a patch of bright pink skin that runs from his jaw line to just under his eyes. The flesh looks like a freshly healing burn, and up close, she can see tiny blemishes of greasy purple skin. She had seen his bright blue eye through the slit, but now she is staring deep into his other eye, pink and black and twitching, withered in its socket. Only the skin around and directly above his blue eye looks human, and it bulges obscenely, as if something is implanted along the eyebrow. The skin around his sickly small eye is black and charred. Deep crimson cracks run the surface of the black skin. Thick green pockets of infection and pus dot the cracks and leak when he tilts his head. His blue eye lights up, and his bottom lip curls into a smile.

At the sight of his face, Karen's knees go weak. Her body slumps toward the floor, twisting the old metal handcuffs into her wrists and tearing hair from her head in thick clumps. He laughs in her face, and his breath is like warm decay on her skin. Her head throbs from all the hair that was pulled out to hang limply from the knots on the fence. Blood runs freely from her scalp and drips off her chin and ears onto her t-shirt. It hurts like hell, but now she can move her head enough to look to her left. She sees a small stairway with a simple metal handrail in the far corner. A second, unseen, window splashes sunlight down across the top few stairs and the few dirty steps signaling a path to freedom. Just knowing freedom is twenty feet away gives Karen hope, and that hope gives her strength to silence her cries and whimpers. She stares at the staircase, and a weak smile forms unintentionally across her blood-streaked face.

Doctor DeFeo follows her gaze and smiles his lipless grin again. "Ahhhh, believe it or not, I've shared both your current view and the feeling of optimism that is surely stirring in your stomach." He turns both eyes on her, but she doesn't return his gaze. She chooses instead to stare at the stairway and indulge the hope she feels. He watches the blood drip down her face and continues. "I died down here. With a vantage point very similar to yours, in fact."

Karen tries in vain to tune DeFeo's deep, wet voice out as he continues. "You called it a *riot*." He shakes his head slowly, then dramatically raises his hands, palms up. "It was an *uprising*. It was a grand and gruesome *insurrection* against the walls that mocked and tormented them and the men dwelling inside those walls."

Doctor DeFeo stands with leathery creaking noises, smiles his demented grin, and twists his head down and to his left and back very rapidly. After the third twist, a popping noise, which sounds almost like bones on metal, echoes off the brick walls. He turns slowly away from her and lifts his arms as he talks and walks in and out of her line of sight.

"It was Dr. Gambrel's blunder, and he would not refute it if you were to inquire of him. You can't, of course, because I killed that sadistic old windbag. I slit his throat so he wouldn't whistle anymore, as a gift to the other fiends that are sure to reside in whatever hell he is scorching in."

Karen still doesn't pull her gaze from the stairway and the light swirling with dust. She feels tears running down from her eyes and sees the blood dripping from her head, but she ignores both to stare at the stairs. She imagines Jay bounding down them and sneaking up on the madman while he rants and raves. She can see him saving her. From the far right of the room, DeFeo shouts, "I didn't kill him by slitting his throat, for *your* record."

His last statement tugs at her natural curiosity, a weakness that led to her fun and exciting job as a reporter for the local paper. Here, in this red-brick basement, she curses it for drawing her attention from the stairway, yet she lets it give her another source of hope. If this madman wants to set his history straight, maybe he will leave her alive to tell the story.

He walks between the shadow-darkened shelves while he asks, "Can you turn your head to the right?"

He doesn't wait for an answer before continuing, "Our office was right through these doors." He points a gloved finger at the shadows to the right of Karen. She strains her eyes, but she sees no door. "Above us, Miss Myers, are two floors formerly occupied by the stark raving mad. The floor directly above us has thick steel bars on the doors and windows, for that's where the most insane lived. The patients overtook their two sentries one temperate spring afternoon. One they hung from the roof, to gag and strangle while a frenzied mob looked on from below, and the other they decapitated and passed around as a hand puppet until someone found his ring of keys on his belt loop. They descended on Dr. Gambrel and me while he was drilling a hole an inch and a half into the side of a convicted murderer's head. The door burst open, and I stood and stared at the slowly advancing mob while Dr. Gambrel coolly and quietly escaped the room. I turned to ask his advice and noticed he'd fled even as the lunatics engulfed me."

He walks slowly with his head down as he steps from behind a shelf and into the ray of sunlight. "They carried me out through those doors and hurled me to the ground. Fists and feet flew at my face and head, and I instinctively curled up only to be kicked in the spine 'til I uncurled and suffered more thrashing. Fingers clawed at my flesh, and teeth drew blood all over. They pulled out my hair in clumps and handfuls and tossed it in the air while they cursed and howled. I tried to crawl away and was pulled back into their midst. I remember blows from clenched fists and bare feet raining down on me until I heard a wet crack and the world tinted brown."

He sits back in the chair across from her. "I swam through gulfs of darkness and madness and turned back around. I woke with a start, hearing sirens in the distance. I opened my eyes, and the world looked different, as if it was starting to decay before my eyes. My mouth was dry, and I couldn't swallow. But I could move. I fanned my fingers, and the bones creaked under my skin. I sat up and the pain in my skull flared, dropping me back to the floor. I crawled to our office and found what was left of the inmate Dr. Gambrel had been drilling. It was a terrible mess; they chopped him and fed him to the incinerator just there to your right." He nods to Karen's right, and she shivers but makes no attempt to follow his nod.

"The pain in my skull faded like a match flame, and within moments, I could stand. I walked down the hall, passing rampaging idiots and crazies, searching for my teacher. I found him curled up, hiding in a janitor closet on the fourth floor. I walked in, and he greeted me with a hug I would have killed for before. He didn't know I was dead, and he bawled for forgiveness for leaving me behind. I saw his face, and his skin melted away, revealing the rot and mold beneath it. I felt no feeling—no anger, no pain, and no sorrow. I felt no joy and no shock; I felt only the cold breath of death. I understood for the first time how he could do the things he did to those people. He was dead like me."

DeFeo claps his hands together softly and lays them on his lap. "A desire rose within me that I haven't yet been able to suppress, and I had to take his life. I took the drill from his stillshaking hands and drove it into the side of his skull. He gagged up blood and defecated all over himself. I realized my mistake when I saw the change in his shocked eyes. I saw his rotten spirit flee his corpse as he fled from the maniacs that killed me. I saw it in his eyes as they turned dull."

He shakes his head slowly and lowers it solemnly. "I dragged his limp form all the way back down to our lab, undisturbed by the madness surrounding me. I laid him on the table he had killed so many on, and I slit his throat. No more whistling. Then I severed his hands. For the evil they had manifested."

The air in the basement feels like it drops ten degrees, but Karen starts sweating. She struggles for words, finds none, and resumes looking at the staircase awaiting sweet Jay. She knows she should be thinking of something to say, something to ease the maniac's troubled mind, but the truth is that the more he speaks, the more she believes who he is and what her fate is to be.

"I admit to you and to these cursed walls that I killed him." He pauses and stands before continuing. "But to call me a *serial killer* is a grave misnomer. I, Miss Myers, am a *doctor*. The only difference between me and the golf-playing doctors of today is that I am *dead,* and I service only the *dead*. And I despise plaid."

He takes a few steps closer and pauses, tilting his head, awaiting an answer to his story. Karen doesn't want to get drawn into any more conversation with DeFeo. She wishes she could go back in time and find a different gory fascination. She doesn't want to answer, but she knows what will happen if she doesn't.

She draws a deep breath and asks, "How can you service the dead?"

He smiles his half-grin and answers smugly, "I give them life, Miss Myers, like I have achieved. Prolonged life when mortality has claimed us. I extend the lease their souls have on their bodies. I am the giver of life to the dead!"

Karen winces at the rising tone of Dr. DeFeo's voice, and she starts weeping involuntarily when she hears heavy thudding footsteps approaching the sunlit stairs. He claps his gloved hands together and tells her excitedly, "Here is my exhibit A, my bodyguard."

As he finishes his sentence, a shirtless mountain of a man lumbers stiffly down the stairs. His muscles bulge and twitch as he turns and faces them. His skin is greenish-gray, and dark brown veins spread like decayed lightning under it. A fine layer of grease or oil seems to coat him. His eyes are sunk back in his skull, and his hair, filthy and blond, hangs in uneven clumps across his forehead and face. He is horribly familiar to Karen, but she can't think of where or when she has seen him before.

"This is my bodyguard. He had it all in life: money, women, and fame. Do you find him familiar?" The doctor walks toward the giant dead man but keeps his eyes trained on a visibly shaken Karen.

She does recognize him, vaguely. His once-handsome face has been carved and mutilated, but the familiar air about him extends beyond his looks and into his entire being. She is positive she's seen him before, but no further details un-cloud in her mind.

DeFeo sees the faraway hint in her eyes, and he continues as he approaches the giant. "He was a gladiator and a showman. This brave undead soldier before you was hailed as a champion, though I understand that the winners of said contests were predetermined. At any rate, they called him 'The Viking Warrior,' and he awed them all with his strength and ferocity!"

Halfway through his long-winded introduction, Karen puts a name to the face. The walking corpse standing before her is none other than Johan Kinderburg or, as DeFeo called him, "The Viking Warrior." Kinderburg was Jay's favorite professional wrestler, and he had died of a rumored drug overdose a few weeks prior. Jay had been devastated in his solemn nerdy way, and she hadn't seen him watching the wrestling shows since he heard the news.

Now, her boyfriend's dead idol lifts a muscular arm to the doctor. Gripped tight in the hand is a twisted strip of duct tape. As he moves, his muscles flex and twitch under his dead skin. Black ooze leaks from angry-looking wounds on his chest and stomach. He pays the wounds no heed, but a smell like formaldehyde seeps out with the ooze, and the smell burns Karen's eyes. She turns her head away from the giant and takes quick shallow breaths, attempting to hold the sickening odor at bay.

"Pardon me a moment, Miss Myers," DeFeo tells her before looking at the dead Kinderburg. The big man is staring at Karen, and a smile twitches at his gray lips. DeFeo stands directly in front of the behemoth and wordlessly slaps him hard across the face. The dead man's head shows no effect of the blow, but his eyes move from Karen to Doctor DeFeo. The doctor smiles his obscene grin and tilts his head at the giant the same way he had with Karen when he awaited an answer. Kinderburg's eyes roll, and he shakes his fist, now wrapped in the duct tape.

"Another?" DeFeo asks him loudly.

The monster's eyes roll back and forth, and he nods his blond head. He grunts and groans and shakes his fist.

"Just one?" DeFeo asks, his head still tilted to the side.

The monster nods.

"Where?" Impatience resonates in his voice.

74

The monster points toward the ceiling, looks at DeFeo, and raises his finger even higher.

"Okay," DeFeo says and takes a step back from the dead giant. "And the cop?"

The giant looks at DeFeo for a second before raising his hand and showing him a streak of bright blue paint on his forearm. The color stands out in strong contrast to the greenishgray of the thing's skin.

"Good." DeFeo claps his hands and looks back to Karen, still talking to Kinderburg. "Take him there. They'll love his company, I'm sure."

DeFeo takes wide, deliberate steps toward Karen, but he still speaks to the retreating giant. "Deposit him, and revisit with haste."

The dead man casts a last hungry look at Karen before he moves slowly and awkwardly up the staircase and out of sight. The hollow thudding of his footsteps echoes in the stairwell and shakes dust from the pipes overhead.

Dr. DeFeo waits for his beast to disappear, and then he rushes Karen, burying his right fist in her stomach. She has no time to flex in anticipation, and the force of the blow cracks three ribs on her left side.

Karen screams, and he slugs her again, this time with his left fist. Her next scream dies into a wet grunt as more ribs flare in agony. She tries her best to block any more blows, but he is backing away, apparently satisfied for the moment.

"Why didn't you tell me you weren't alone?" He tilts his head at her, fury burning in his blue eye. Karen realizes with a shudder in her soul that the giant dead man has found Jay.

She answers before she can stop herself. "Wasn't it in the 'diminutive notebook' you got from the detectives?"

He smiles at her. Dark drool slips from his purple bottom lip. "The notebook was hardly in any condition to read thoroughly. And the same could honestly be said for the peace officers themselves. They put up a good battle and even managed to get a few shots off at my bodyguard. Wretchedly for them, bullets don't have much effect unless they are directed at the cranium. My giant tore them apart."

The grin never falters as he goes on. "Literally, he tore them apart. I spent the majority of my morning putting them back together again. I believe I accomplished more with those officers of the law than all the king's horses and all the king's men accomplished with Humpty Dumpty." He snickers to himself. "I had to put them together, my first ever two-souled zombie. An experiment, to be sure, but they woke and ate the remains of their individuality as it lay splattered on the tiled floor. They always wake so hungry."

Karen hears DeFeo speaking, but her mind is stuck on Jay, wherever he may be, and she can follow little of what the madman is saying. At the same time, she doesn't want to call any more of his anger down on herself, and she tries her best to fake attentiveness. The doctor walks in long strides back and forth in front of her, glaring at her with his mismatched eyes. She feels his anger as if it radiates off him in the cool of the basement.

At a loss for words again, she simply cries, "Why?"

"Why?" he asks back. "Because I see through the eyes of the dead. I burned my eye to stop seeing it. I carved the nose from my face to avoid the bittersweet smell of decay you living souls emit. In reality, the world is already full of the walking dead. I just plan on raising an army of them and making this world die. Making the rot a reality, you could say.

"I make the educated guess that 'how' will be your next question, and allow me to answer that as simply as I can." DeFeo takes a deep breath and explains as if he is talking to a child, "I use a bastardized mix of science and godless heathen magic to raise them. A little shock to the brainstem, the right mix of herbs and poisons, and up the dead stand, ready to feast and serve. I admit it takes precious time to raise just one, and their appetites are indeed voracious, but I've figured out how to give them life. How devilishly ironic is that, the dead giving the dead life?"

He laughs, loud and confident, inches from her face. "I've been a host of disproportionate manners, and I've answered all your whimpered queries. So now, Karen Myers, answer my question."

His breath is hot and foul on her face, and she recoils instinctively. The corners of his mouth curl upward, and he softly rubs the back of a gloved hand across her face. "Why would college students study me? And please, for your own sake and well-being, be honest with me."

Karen feels a last desperate hope in his curiosity, and she answers him honestly. "I was studying psychological disorders in college. According to all the available history of DeFeo ..." After a worried glance to the head-tilting madman, she amends her words. "*You,* I mean. *You* believe you are dead when you aren't." DeFeo folds his hands in front of him and nods at her. She feels hope slipping away, but she continues regardless. "I argued that you suffered from Cotard's Syndrome, or Walking Corpse Syndrome as it is more commonly known."

DeFeo's one blue eye seems to quiver with anger, but she can't stop herself. "With Cotard's, the victims experience such strong feelings of detachment that they believe they have become deceased. There are other people like you, doctor, other people who feel the same. We can find you help."

He hunches forward and massages his temple with one hand, "No," he says while reaching for his razor blade. "NO ONE feels what I feel, or rather what I don't feel. And NO ONE can help. Not me, not your doomed lover, and certainly not you."

With that, he slashes the razor in front of him, and with a whisper of the blade, a paper-thin crimson line becomes visible across Karen's pale throat. She gasps for air that forces thick droplets of blood out of her slit throat and goes no farther. He takes a step back and tilts his head as her blood gushes from her throat and down her body to the floor. She speaks no more words, but small groans and grunts escape her dying lips as he disappears into the shadows. He reappears quickly with an ancient gurney. He rolls it next to her. As her world goes black, he is reaching up and cutting her hair from the fence.

## X

Jay watches the two-headed monster carefully. It stands in the corner opposite him in front of the thin, arched window. A row of gray-bricked casements line the wall, each painted a different bold color. Red, green, pink, and yellow shine bright as the sun kisses them. The monster stands between the last two windows, the left hand painting one window blue and the right hand painting the last orange. Each head seems to be focused solely on the window in front of it. Every now and then, one of the two heads moans softly, and Jay shifts in his chair, unable to scream because of the duct tape across his mouth.

He doesn't know how long he has been sitting here, ducttaped to a chair. His mind has twisted from everything he has been through over the past several hours. He wonders if the terrible things he is seeing are real or if his perception of reality has been somehow permanently warped. The night started ominously when Karen demanded to visit the abandoned grounds of the Medford Hospital for the Criminally Insane. Jay felt dread thick and nervous in his stomach as they walked the shadows of the empty buildings. Two half-frantic detectives rushed them to the back of the administration building with guns drawn and told them to leave. Karen grabbed him by the hand and was leading them away from the eerie grounds when a giant gray-skinned man stepped from the shadows and slugged Karen in her temple. She crashed into Jay, and he fell into the shadows, hitting his head on the red brick wall. The two cops came running, and Jay heard a few pops of gunfire before he faded into blackness, his last thoughts about Karen.

The morning sunlight was creeping across the vacant grounds when he came to. A screaming pain radiated from a three-inch gash on the back of his head, but his thoughts cleared fast. He realized right away that Karen, the two cops, and their giant attacker were all gone. For only the tiniest instant did leaving the cursed place occur to him, for he couldn't leave without Karen. Life simply wouldn't be worth living without her. He was drawn to the main building, and he crept through the ever-shrinking shadows to avoid the monster from the night before. There was no opening the door, but the ground-floor windows were all simple red plank boards, and the first one he kicked splintered under his work boots.

He shimmied through the window and into a cold, tilefloored room. The door was swung wide open, and sunlight shone the color of a rotting pear in the hallway. He snuck down the hallway, bathed in that gruesome light, peeking in darkened rooms as he went. Every shadow menaced, and every creak sounded like thunder in the desolate hallways. On the stairway leading to the second floor, he bumped into the giant that stole away Karen. Jay beat his fists against the man's cold oily skin, but the man stood unaffected. Recognition dawned as to whom he was punching right as the behemoth wrapped his large hands around his throat. For the second time in a matter of hours, Jay plunged into darkness at the hands of the gray-skinned giant. Before he faded, he wondered what kind of nightmare it was when your dead favorite wrestler strangled you in an abandoned building.

A loud creak from down the hall outside the room brings Jay back into his twisted reality. The right side of the monster stops painting and turns toward the sound. Enough sunlight splashes across his mangled face for Jay to recognize him as one of the cops from earlier. The left head ignores the right head and the sound and clumsily dips the seven-inch brush in its hand into a gallon of blue paint on a table next to it. Jay turns to see a horribly scarred man limping quickly down the hall toward him. Black hair swings in knots across the man's face and hangs

81

wild on his shoulders. Jay only sees one eye, and it is brilliant blue. The other seems shadowed. The man holds one gloved finger to his mouth, which is missing the upper lip, as he approaches. Jay wants to scream at the man in the hallway, wants to scream at the two-headed cop and his undead idol, wants to scream himself sane at the horror of the whole night. He tries, but the duct tape across his mouth muffles the sound so that it offers no release. Fear and frustration bubble over, and big salty tears roll down
Jay's face.

The man slows his step as he enters the room and turns to observe the two-headed painter. He watches the monster for a second before the right side sobs and moans. The man says nothing, but his mouth curls in a hideous grin. He raises his finger a second time to silence Jay. Jay responds by shaking his head and letting his eyes roll wild in their sockets. The disfigured man walks silently across the tile floor, casting glances at the twoheaded zombie until he circles behind Jay. Black-gloved hands rest on Jay's shoulder as the man leans close to his ear.

His rank breath makes Jay recoil against his duct-tape bonds as the man whispers in a deep, wet voice, "My name is Doctor Benjamin Clyde DeFeo."

The man spins a second dusty chair and places it in front of Jay with a crash. Both of the monster's heads turn to face the noise. The thing takes a clumsy step forward into the sunlight, and Jay sees with terrible detail that both cops have been sewn together. The left head stares at DeFeo with fear in its dead eyes. The right head howls at the sight of DeFeo. The force of the guttural sound sends blood and spit across the room. The left head cowers, a look of fear etched on its gray face. DeFeo claps his hands together and turns his full attention to the monstrosity.

His voice booms in the wide room. "Hello, my child."

The right head roars at DeFeo with even more fury than before. The head shakes and pulls away from the cowering left head so hard that Jay sees thick staples between the two heads ooze black goo. The right side of the monster takes a long, clumsy step. The left stays frozen, and the monster sways in the waning sunlight. The right head howls in frustration and then faces the left and roars. The left groans and leans back and away from the other head.

DeFeo shakes his head. "Your souls are rejecting each other. I hypothesized that, since you were partners in enforcing the law, you would be well suited for this experiment." His black hair sways when he shakes his head again. "I was *wrong*."

Something about the way DeFeo says the word "wrong" sends the right side into an even greater fury. The two sides of the zombie pull and tug away from each other. The right head wants to attack DeFeo, and the left wants to flee from him. They both groan and howl as staples pop and tear with spurts of dark ooze. The left hand reaches back and grabs the paintbrush it had been using. The right is still screaming hoarsely at DeFeo, and it doesn't notice the other head until it rams the handle of the paintbrush into its ear. The terrible scream winds down to a wet gurgle, and the right side goes limp, pulling the left to the floor with it. The monster lands with a crash on the tile floor. The left head moans and cries, unable to move other than to slam its arm into the floor repeatedly.

DeFeo turns to Jay, and the lipless man tells him, "I truly expected it to do better than *this*." He sighs empathetically. "Experiments fail as well as succeed."

The left side of the zombie moans and scratches at the floor as if he is trying to crawl. DeFeo turns away from the immobile dead thing and circles back behind Jay. He grabs the back of the chair and turns it with an ear-piercing shriek so Jay is facing a wall with tattered and stained wallpaper hanging from it.

"I already feel like a terrible host," DeFeo explains from behind him. "You are in my house. You've watched my children die, and I still don't know your name. The least I can do is to offer you a slight respite from what I am obliged to now do."

Terrified and confused, Jay turns and looks over his shoulder as far as his bonds allow. He watches DeFeo dig in a pocket inside his long black coat. He pulls from the shadows of his coat an almost comically large hypodermic needle. He reaches down and softly rubs the left head's hair like any other loving father would. A wicked grin

84

spreads across his deformed face, and he slams the huge needle into the side of the head he is cradling. DeFeo pulls the head back in an arch as he injects strange orange goo into the zombie's head. The zombie's eyes turn from yellow and white to crimson so dark it looks black. The doctor drops the head, and it lands with a plop in the gathering puddle of black slime leaking out the right head's ear.

With a sigh, DeFeo says, "Remedied and noted."

He grabs Jay's chair and spins him halfway back around. He raises his hand and rips the duct tape off Jay's face in one quick movement. DeFeo settles back in the chair he'd positioned before the ordeal with the two-headed monster.

"And now on to you." He holds up his hands as if to allow Jay to speak.

"Why are you doing this?" Jay manages before he begins to sob uncontrollably.

"God's wounds!" DeFeo stands to his feet and shakes his hands in front of him. "I must inform you, nameless sir, that I have already been reminded once today why the dead prefer the companionship of the dead, and I am not inclined to take a subsequent lesson."

He leans within kissing distance of Jay's face. Up close, Jay can see the second eyeball, black and pink and withered. Jay takes a deep scared breath, and he smells the blood and burnt flesh of DeFeo. He wants to gag but fights the urge so as not to anger the mad doctor.

The heavy, thudding footfalls of the "Viking Warrior" echo from the hallway along with a faint, but distinct, squeaking noise. Jay tries to turn to see what could possibly be coming next in his nightmare. DeFeo reaches up and slaps Jay's face before grabbing and squeezing it. His hot breath makes Jay's eyes feel dry and sandy.

"Don't be rude. Answer my inquiry. What … is … your …name?"

The giant's footfalls are nearly to the room, and Jay recognizes the squeak sound as a small wheel that needs lube. He knows the dead wrestler is pushing something into the room, but DeFeo won't let him turn his head.

Tears fall from Jay's eyes and run into DeFeo's gloves, soaking into the thick leather. "Jay," he manages despite DeFeo's grip on his face.

"Your name is a letter? Ridiculous," DeFeo snorts.

DeFeo loosens his grip on Jay's face, but when Jay turns to look, as the footsteps and squeaks stop behind him, DeFeo slaps him a second time.

Still within inches of Jay's face, DeFeo asks, "Why are you here?"

Jay calms himself at the thought of Karen. She is his strength. He imagines the smell of her sandy hair and the feeling of her naked flesh, and he tells DeFeo, "I came here last night with my girlfriend, Karen."

DeFeo snorts, and a fine mist of blood puffs from the crater where his nose should be. Tiny pinprick blood drops dot Jay's face in its wake. DeFeo grabs Jay's face twice as hard as before. He reaches his other hand to the giant. He pulls back a length of duct tape, which he uses to cover Jay's mouth, despite his pleas and cries.

DeFeo shakes his head and tells Jay, "I've met Karen, Jay. She is a lovely lady, but a terrible conversationalist." He smiles a twisted grin at Jay, who squirms from it.

"I think she may have a bit of a crush on me," DeFeo says behind the lipless smile. "Did you know she studied me in college?"

DeFeo turns his withered pink eye at Jay, and Jay nods frantically.

"She is curious about me. I'm a god, dear boy, so who could cast the blame on her for being mortal?"

The question confuses Jay, but he answers what he thinks DeFeo wants to hear and shakes his head "no" back and forth.

The smile fades from DeFeo's mangled face, and Jay feels his end fast approaching. He thinks of Karen and his family and his youth and his everything. He closes his eyes and lets it all flash like a movie behind his eyelids until DeFeo slaps him hard a third time.

"I'm glad you agree," DeFeo tells him coldly before grabbing the chair and turning back to face the giant and what he has brought.

The giant stands blocking the dim light from behind him, but even in the growing shadows, Jay sees Karen sitting in the wheelchair in front of him. Her head is tilted to one side as if resting on her shoulder. Her skin is a greasy gray, and Jay screams behind his gag when he sees the crimson smile across her pale throat. Thick dark stitches hold the wound closed in tiny x marks.

"I will take her under my wing and teach her more than she knew was possible. You, my poor friend, will serve as so many fine lessons for her."

DeFeo leans close to a motionless Karen and rubs the back of his hand across her cheek. She blinks her yellow eyes and leans slowly toward the doctor. A growl rumbles from her throat, and DeFeo smiles as he backs up. He claps his hands, and the dead giant leans the wheelchair forward until he dumps Karen to the floor. She stares at Jay with yellow-and-white eyes as she begins to crawl toward him with great effort, dragging her legs.

DeFeo looks at Jay and nods with the madding grin. "She remembers."

Karen grabs the cuff of Jay's pants and pulls until she can seize his other ankle with a cold hand. She reaches from his cuff to his knee and from his ankle to his thigh. Her nails dig into Jay's skin as she pulls herself up between his legs. She rests her breasts on Jay's knees; her mouth is opening and closing as if she is trying to talk, but no sound can be heard. Doctor DeFeo clasps his hands on Jay's shoulders and leans to his ear as Karen reaches one hand up, sinking her nails deep into his thigh. Blood stains his jeans and leaks to the floor as her nails sever his femoral artery. She reaches with her other hand and grabs his stomach, and she pulls herself closer.

DeFeo whispers, "She remembers her first lesson."

Karen snaps forward, tearing at Jay's throat. His world fades into the sunlight and the colors of the windows. The last thing he hears besides Karen's chewing and DeFeo telling him, "They always wake up hungry," is the sound of his own dying heartbeat.

# CORPSE EATER

Even though he is fairly new to the mortician game, Marty Newstead has a deep and dismal feeling rolling in his gut as he walks up the staircase to the Stillwater Funeral Home. He tells himself it is first-day jitters coupled with the fact that his chosen profession is the personification of macabre to most people. Not to mention, he was actually called in a night early due to an emergency in Dry Hill, forty-five minutes down mountain. It is Marty's first night, and he's going to be flying solo while the head mortician sees to the emergency out of town.

A series of small ornate lamps light the wide stone steps, and the porch light above the door casts long shadows from the potted trees that line the large porch. An old stone archway surrounds the door, and an ominous gargoyle glares down at Marty from its apex. The darkened building looks like the bastard child of a lumber factory and a Victorian mansion, with the basement and rear of the building used for the town's mortuary and morgue, and the front being the elegant funeral home complete with a room large enough to handle any funeral for the surrounding area. It is a damn big building for a lot of little towns. It looms over the nearby houses, most of which are decrepit and empty, and the long brick chimney from the basement even towers over a few of the two-hundred-year-old pines that shade the town. Marty knocks, and the face that answers is a sharp contrast to the gloomy aura hanging over the property.

"Hello, Mr. Newstead. Thank you so much for helping me out here."

Niles "Ripper" Jensen, the head mortician, opens the door wide to let Marty in. Having only spoken to Ripper, as he swore his friends called him, over the phone, Marty immediately relaxes when he sees the man is only a year or two out of college himself. He isn't an inch over five feet tall, but his smile is so big and genuine that it actually makes him seem taller. His two-inch platform boots help with that as well. Ripper's dark hair is short and slicked back, and his tattooed forearms are vibrant against the stark white of his smock. He notices Marty looking, and he nods.

"I see ya checking out my ink," Ripper says and steps closer as he rolls up his smock sleeve to his shoulder. "I got a guy in Falterwood that does sick work. Ha! Two morticians talking about sick work!"

He cracks himself up with his joke, and Marty can't help but chuckle along.

"I think we'll get along fine," Ripper says with a nod. Then, "Let me give ya the quickie tour so I can bounce down to Dry Hill and stuff that stiff. Hopefully I can be back within the next two hours and help you with the tripleheader shotgun homicide you got waitin' on ya downstairs!"

The dismal feeling tugs at Marty's gut again. His eyes widen, and his nervous smile wanes. Ripper's smile doesn't.

"HA! I'm just fucking with you, new kid. Ya only got two, and neither one is a shotgun. Ya got an old-age we gotta cook and a rock climber with a broken fucking neck. Hey, you like
Metallica?"

Marty laughs despite his nervousness.

"Yeah, I guess."

Ripper leads Marty through a nice hallway decorated with hundreds of photos and a few large wood-framed mirrors. He walks to a curtain-covered wall and slides the dark green curtains to the side, revealing metal double doors. He turns back to Marty as he opens the door.

"They had a bassist named Jason Newstead after bass god Cliff Burton died in a bus crash. So the rest of the band always called Newstead 'New Kid.' I think years of it finally fucking got to him, 'cuz he fucking bounced. He left Metallica, one of the biggest fucking metal bands ever! You ain't gonna bounce if I call ya New Kid, are ya?"

Ripper's easy nature does its best to calm Marty's nervous stomach. When Marty laughs, it is sincere but still shaky with nervousness.

"Nah, I need the money."

"Right on," Ripper grins. "Well, this up here is the funeral home."

He waves a small tattooed arm around the dark room.

"We'll check it out when I'm not in a hurry. It's creepy and old and smells like death, so, if you're like me, you'll dig it." He pushes, and the doors open with a squeal that echoes around the two men. He nods toward the staircase and allows Marty past. As he lets the door shut, he tells him, "The party's down here!"

Ripper gives Marty a rushed tour with as many facts about mid-eighties and -nineties thrash bands as about the simple necessities for taking care of tonight's two bodies. Ripper catches sight of his watch midway through the tour and says, "Shit! I gotta get the hell outta here. Hey, listen man, be sure to get old man Vickerson cooking before you start slicing on the clumsy climber, all right? It's an old-ass oven, and we gotta warm that son of a bitch up, so set a timer. Wait for it and make sure he's cooking before you're cutting. Important!" "Okay." Marty nods.

"All right. I'll hurry back. Hopefully we can bond over gutting up that broken neck. You got any questions, New Kid?"

"Yeah, a few."

"Well, ask fast."

"I've never seen a funeral home owned by the city. Is that common around here?"

"Nope. The place used to be called the Baxter Family Funeral Home, but something happened and the town took it over. Next."

"How long have you been working here?"

"About ten months. They have a hell of a time keeping morticians around here. I'll explain later on. Just remember: cook before cut!"

Ripper smiles, grabs his coat and bounds up the stairs two at a time. Marty hears his footfalls across the ceiling above him, and the dismal feeling in his gut stirs in the silence that follows. He convinces himself that this is what he signed on for, and he sets about his work. He walks into the crematorium and sets the faded old knob timer on the ancient furnace. Marty has been in crematoria before, and none has ever reeked like this one. A strong strange chemical smell lingers alongside the typical burntdeath smell of such old ovens. Marty shivers but thinks of how nice a paycheck will be. He shuts the door to the crematorium and thinks of how much he'll enjoy paying off some of his school loans. How good it will feel to show his dad that he can make money at his chosen trade.

Marty takes a small walk in the rooms through which he had been rushed moments before. He makes mental notes of what tools are kept where. He makes a mental map of the basement, and as he lays out the tools he'll need for the climber, he hums a funeral dirge. Marty pulls both men out of their cold drawers, placing the climber on the steel table and Mr. Vickerson on a steel gurney so he can wheel him into the oven. He looks at his watch and tells the old man's corpse, "That should be long enough to cook your skinny ass, old fella."

He pushes the gurney down the small fluorescent-lit hallway, still whistling his dark melody. His slams the gurney into the door, and it swings open with a clatter. Marty gags as he follows the gurney into the room. The chemical smell burns his eyes and throat, but he can see through his sudden tears that the door to the cremator is wide open. Black slime drips boiling down the side and pools at its base. Clumps of ash litter the floor and stick to the chemical-reeking slime. Marty covers his mouth and nose and squints through watery eyes at the temperature gauge. He moans in frustration when he sees it isn't nearly as hot as it needs to be to reduce old man Vickerson to little gray ash balls yet. Marty slams the door to the cremator shut and double-checks the timer. He pushes the gurney holding Vickerson to the side of the room and decides to get a start on cutting up the climber.

The chemical smell hits Marty like a poke in the eye when he opens the door to the hallway. A strange dragging trail of the black ash-covered slime leads down the hallway toward the room with the dead climber in it. The steel door swings lightly, waving the chemical odor back down the hall at Marty. He freezes one step outside the door to the crematorium and pulls his cell phone from his apron. He dials Ripper's cell phone and takes a slow step forward.

Wet tearing sounds echo from the room ahead. The phone rings, and Marty takes another step.

A monstrous snarl, then a second, more intense, tearing sound echo ahead. The phone rings again, and Marty wagers two more steps.

Gulping sounds twist Marty's stomach, but his natural and morbid curiosity has him taking steps even as the phone rings again.

Ripper answers his phone, and all Marty can hear at first is a few lines from Testament's "Return to Serenity." The volume decreases as the line disintegrates to static. The sick feeling prompts Marty to take a few steps back from the door ahead and whisper into the phone.

"Uh, Mr. Jensen ... err, Ripper, this is Marty."

Static crackles the connection, and Ripper shouts into Marty's ear.

"New Kid! Hey, I'm on my way back. The line is breaking up something fierce, everything 'ite?"

Marty tries to tell him something is wrong with the crematorium, but the line buzzes and crackles before dying. Marty curses while closing his phone. More disgusting noises echo out of the cadaver room: snarls, slurps, chewing, and tearing sounds.

The sick feeling rolls and clenches Marty's stomach, but he is walking back toward the door, his stubborn mind sharp against his weak stomach.

*A prank,* he thinks to himself. *That Ripper dude is hazing me.*

Marty reaches the door and places one hand inches from it.

*Just get this over with. No gory little prank is going to scare you away from this job. Tighten that tummy up, and show this prick you don't spook at the sight of a little gore.*

Marty takes one last breath in a feeble attempt to calm his twisting gut before he pushes the door wide open. The chemical reek is stronger than it was in the crematorium or the hallway, and it makes Marty swoon and his eyes blur. He covers his mouth and nose with one hand and wipes the tears from his weeping eyes with his other.

Perched on top of the steel table with the climber's corpse is a humanoid creature with both its arm hidden in the dead body's chest cavity. Its face is half black and half pink, with small bristles poking over all the blackened flesh. The jaw, lined with tiny sharp teeth, hangs wide open—three times as wide as any human could open his mouth—and dribbles the chemical slime onto the body below it, where it sizzles the cold dead flesh. The creature's rail-thin body is covered in the same black bristly skin where there aren't patches of white fabric burnt to the flesh. The thing has its long slender legs tucked under it, and its spindly arms flex as they dig in the corpse. Marty notices that the corpse's legs are chewed and mangled stumps at both knees. The feeling in his stomach is turning into something sour creeping up his throat.

The thing turns its glowing orange eyes on Marty. Marty backs into the doorway, smacking his head on the steel. The creature opens its mouth impossibly wide and screeches at Marty, spraying him with chunks of cold gore. The thing pulls two handfuls of gray-and-pink organs from the cadaver's chest and gorges on them with brutal chewing and slurping sounds. Marty screams like he has never screamed before. The creature responds by hurling a handful of mashed dead guts at the screaming man. The ground-up organs hit Marty in his chest. His stomach, solid steel through all of his schooling, heaves, and Marty vomits his dinner down his gore-soaked smock. The thing stands on the table but has to duck to keep from hitting the low ceiling. It reaches a clawed hand back into the chest for more goodies. As it pulls at the corpse's innards, the cadaver jerks and tears. The beast stuffs the last handful of cold guts into its mouth and dives at Marty. Marty sees the thing leap toward him but it moves too fast for him to run away. He raises his arms to cover his face, he smells the chemical reek, and his knees go weak. The monster slams through the door next to Marty and, relieved, Marty lets the darkness take him.

The first thing Marty hears when he starts to come to is Exodus's "Bonded by Blood" blaring from the small beat-up CD player Ripper keeps next to his work table.

Marty opens his eyes slowly and silently scans the room. Ripper is singing along to the classic thrash album with his back to Marty while he works on the climber's dead body. Marty leans up, feels the wet throb on the back of his head, notices his gore- and vomit-covered smock, and groans.

Ripper turns around with an impish grin.

"Good morning, New Kid. Some crazy shit go down? Or are you just a shitty mortician?"

"No," Marty says while rubbing the goose egg on his head. The memory of the corpse-eating monster is vivid and surreal, and he tells Ripper, "Something was eating him. Holy shit, it was the most fucked-up thing I've ever seen." "And it scared you so bad you passed out?"

"Well, yeah. I thought it was gonna eat me."

"Nah, you ain't dead. It ate half of Vickerson before I scared it back into the oven when I got back. Shit, New Kid, I already had to catch a coupla' alley cats to fill up his urn. Damn lucky this town is swarming with strays, huh?"

"You knew about that *thing?*"

"Yeah, I shoulda' told you about all this." Ripper looks at the half-devoured corpse on the table, takes off his latex gloves, and tosses them into the trash. He sits on the floor next to Marty.

"That was old man Baxter. The guy the funeral home used to be named after."

"Is this a sick joke? Because I don't think it's funny." Now that terror is passing, anger is replacing it in Marty's shocked mind.

"Nope. No joke. Let me tell you a quick little story, 'ite?"

Unable to tell if he is being had or not, Marty just says, "Fine."

Ripper stands up and offers Marty a hand, which he takes. Marty sways on weak knees and notices that Ripper has resewn the corpse closed and even dressed it in its burial clothes. The legless pants hang limply off the side of the table. The chemical smell still lingers lightly in the air, but Ripper has mopped up the ash and slime.

"So, about sixty years ago, Chuck Baxter ran this place. His great-granddaddy opened it and ran it for years. The building and the profession were passed down through the Baxter family until old Chuck there. Well, somewhere along the line, Chuck's brain warped, and he decided he enjoyed the taste of cold dead meat. No one knows how long he had been cutting off pieces of the bodies he worked on, but one hot summer day, the whole town found out."

"How?'

"Well, they were burying a sweet little girl named Cindy Maskiss, and after the viewing but before the actual burial, her momma snuck in and lifted the coffin lid to give her baby girl one last goodbye. Instead, she saw the corpse of her daughter with stumps where her legs should have been. Her reaction was immediate and severe. As was that of the funeral party. The people, already grief-stricken and distraught, attacked the morbid mortician and dragged him down here. Men, women, and children beat him with fists, feet, and table legs. They dragged him to the embalming room and held him down while they stuck tubes down his throat, up his ass, and in his ears. The entire funeral party stood and howled while they pumped the stillliving Baxter full of deadly chemicals."

"Damn."

"Yeah, damn, but they still weren't done yet. They carried his twitching, smoking body to the crematorium and tossed him into the oven alive. They laughed and hugged as the villain screamed in ungodly agony right there next to them all. The story goes that he was still screaming and moaning at intervals when the place emptied out. The city took over the property, and it became one of those things the people never talk about. All that wasn't enough though, 'cuz the creepy old bastard still sneaks out of the crematorium for midnight snacks every now and then. That's why no one wants to work here. I can't say I blame them; watching him eat is just fucking nasty, and I'm a morbid dude. I cleaned it all up this time, but now that you're working here too, I ain't cleaning up after his crazy ass all the time. You hear me? You got next, New Kid."

"Yeah."

"So you're staying on?"

"Yeah, I need the cash."

The two share an awkward smile at their dark secret.

Marty sighs and asks,

"So what do we do now?"

Ripper stands up, adjusts the tie on the legless corpse, and tells Marty, "Now, we just pray no one checks to make sure this guy is wearing his favorite climbing shoes."

# HUMAN AS A VULTURE

A travesty of warped metal and shattered glass with a scorched rubber tail is ahead and to your left. Someone's day lies smoldering and dying in the belly of the beast. A siren sounds behind you, and screams from your future ring in your ears.

Traffic slows to take it in. Taillights in front of you glow red, angry at your impatience.

Everyone gets their chance to pass the tangled wreckage.

One eye on the road and one on disaster.

Now, your turn is upon you.

The essence of humanity lies in your lingering stare.

# DISASTERNOON

We slept 'til noon because we are both ugly in the morning. We woke up and dragged ourselves from the darkness of my bedroom to the melancholy of my living room. The curtains are drawn over boarded-up windows.

She tells me she's an actress. Maybe she pretends she is someone else when the strobe lights are sweating her and she wraps her legs around the pole. Her lie makes us even, because I told her she was safe.

"I have hopes and dreams," she tells me because she can't stop lying.

I don't trust her limp, because it catches me off guard. Physical frailty makes me nervous, and she misinterprets the apathy etched on my face. She doesn't like my whiskey breath, because it reminds her of her dad.

She turns on the stereo and sweeps her arms across my coffee table. Cigarette butts flee their ashtray tombs, and papers that used to mean something scatter all around. She climbs on the table and dances with tears streaming down her sunken cheeks.

"I can get low," she tells me, and then proves it by slapping her bare ass against the table.

I cradle my whiskey bottle breakfast close to my chest to watch her as tears birthed from our hellish reality scorch my eyes. The dance is jerky, awkward, and sexy, but it doesn't match the funeral dirge blasting from the stereo at all. The morning was a waste, and now the afternoon is a disaster.

# BONE HOME

The air is hot and dry. And still. Yet watch how the curtains sway in that room above the breakfast nook. I'll tell you what makes those ragged drapes dance: spirits, dark and tortured.

Hold my hand, my dear, as we walk the grim halls and rotted rooms of Bone Home.

No, my love, the house is built of wood and nails, wire and glass, as houses often are. The name comes from the man who built this magnificent dwelling. In 1904, Edward Bone carved a clearing in these beautiful pines and built his family a home. Old Edward Bone was a distant cousin to my grandma. By a strange stroke of luck and diminished family bloodline, I now hold the deed. A logger by trade, he knew the wood and used only the best. Edward Bone took nearly every piece of handcrafted furniture and stacked it in some hideous monolith the townsfolk burned. Before we enter, see there where the grass is blackened even after a century's worth of snow and sun? Now into the house itself we venture. This door was handcrafted by artisans long dead and never recognized. It whines and creaks when we open it, but it has done its duty and kept the elements out. We can leave

106

it open if you like, but I think it will be futile; *they* like the door closed. Why allow a breeze if you can't feel it on your face?

To your left, my dear, are the dining room and kitchen. If you look at the dismal gray paper where it still clings to the walls, you can make out the faintest tint of the dark autumn yellow of sunflowers. How cheerful it must have been. Broken dishes and a feeling of nervousness that hangs in the air and clings to your skin are all that remain in the kitchen. The morning sun shines through this big window, and the family would sit at this table to eat breakfast and greet each new day together. No, my dear, blood dries brown. I don't know what has left the smeared black stain across the tabletop. But I can show you century-old blood if we go back to the foyer.

See, my love, they closed the door when we went to the dining room. Before we go upstairs, see that dark blotch. A bloodstain. A deep, old bloodstain. Edward Bone took a baling hook to his oldest daughter, Catherine, and gutted her right where you are standing. She bled out here. She lay in a puddle of her wet innards until her blood soaked into the floorboards and caked to her pale face. Catherine hates this foyer now. She lives in the cellar where her young blood dripped. I can show her to you if you want. She sits and rocks in the corner, trying to keep herself together.

Okay, my dear, there's more to see, so we'll just keep moving. The stairs creak and moan like the dead, but they'll grant us safe passage to the rooms up here. Notice how the pictures still hang on this decrepit wall. Look closer and see how the images are blurred and burned behind the flawless glass. I've stared into the distorted eyes of the images, and I feel them screaming in my head, so, please, limit your glances.

Yes, my love, more blood awaits atop the stairs. Such wonderful tools those loggers used. Edward Bone caved in his son Simon's skull with the five-pound hammer that he used to knock stubborn branches from downed logs, and then stripped him naked like a cedar here in the hallway. Shush, my dear, there is Simon now. He is watching us with his eye. Don't stare at the pulp that his skull is now, for he may take offense. See how his naked form shimmers in the shadows as he sulks into his mother's sitting room.

This, my love, is Edward Bone's wife, Delores Bone. I find her here most often, rocking in her chair as you see her now. Sometimes Pamela, the middle daughter, crowds close, but she is shy around new people. She carries her head in her hands, and her long, beautiful hair is eternally tangled with her blood. Delores can't see you, because, as you can see, he has sewn her eyes shut, but she can hear you. She sings young Simon haunting lullabies to calm his terrified spirit. Her voice is distant and sorrowful; see how it raises the gooseflesh on my arm.

That deep chill and pungent stench, my dear, is Edward drawing close. Watch how Mother Bone and son

108

fade as the murderous patriarch approaches. We will meet him halfway when we turn the tarnished knob to the door to our right.

I must warn you, my love, if old dead Edward Bone speaks, we must cover our ears and leave. I'll open the door now. It creaks loudest of all, and the house vibrates softly as his evil condenses to form a physical being. His restless murderous spirit rolls and swirls, and that, my dear, is what makes the curtains wave. See how they whip now as his apparition appears. Today he is holding the gore-stained hammer and smiling like the damned. He died of starvation here in this room. He slaughtered his family and never again left this house.

Don't look at his dark eyes as they roll in their sockets!

*Ia. Tahgen noob fhtagn. Ia Ia.*

No! My love, cover your ears and back away!

*Ia! Tahgen noob fhtagn! IA! IA! IA!*

My DEAR, my LOVE!

*IA! TAHGEN NOOB FHTAGN! IA! IA! IA! IA!*

I can't save you, my love, and the hammer is all too real now. Your blood drips down my face, and my apology is stuck in my throat. I told you not to listen.

I have to leave now, my dear, but I always return. You'll meet the young daughters Bone now and share in their phantom state—mutilated beauty surround by molding decay. I'll bring you more friends until this house feels alive again.

Maybe, my love, I'll move in so we can always be together in the grim hallways and rotted rooms of Bone Home.

# THE MAN WITH THE ZAFTIG GRIN

"So this is the dying," says the man with the zaftig grin as he fingers the frayed bullet hole in his tummy with one meaty finger.

His smile is chubby and curly, good natured and dishonest. It's the kind of smile that tips over beers and ashtrays at parties. The kind of smile that overstays its welcome habitually.

It's an inside joke and an insult and something you can't forget.

*It never wanes.*

Blood bubbles over his hefty lips to trickle down chin insignificant. His eyes, rendered glossy and distant, roll behind flittering bruised eyelids. His sees his past in between blinks of his present.

(He expects all flowers and regret.)

Nicotine-yellowed curtains slapping against cheap wood paneling.

His fingers wiggling in the air.

Colors so vivid and simple that even forgotten children can remember them.

111

He smells the chlorine burn of betrayal mingled with the gunmetal flavor of his blood. His lungs deflate, but his smile refuses to cease for such a thing as death.

The colors blink with the darkness; the past blinks with the present.

He does his best to focus his blurry eyes on the stillsmoking gun barrel and the cold bitch wielding it. If he could speak without vomiting blood, he would tell her how impressed he was that she handled the .454 so well.

He hopes his smile (his inside joke and insult and something you can't forget) relays his beaming pride. It really only comes across as eerily satisfied.

"When you die, I'm gonna chew that smile off your face," says his wife, the woman with the hirsute frown.

# ALL THAT GLIMMERS ISN'T COPPER

*Main Labor Yard, Hellgate Prison, Conn., 1798*

Behind the twenty-foot-tall rock-and-brick walls of Hellgate Prison, three dozen prisoners are all hammering large chunks of granite. The men grunt and swear as they swing their state-issued sledgehammers, chipping away at the stone and filling the air with a harsh, abrasive powder. The warm summer breeze carries the dust up over the wall through the lush greens of the forested hillside around the distant former copper mine and current prison. The sound of the hammers striking the stone and breaking little piece by little piece away rings and echoes off the walls as it smothers any sound of the nature surrounding them. The dozen guards with eyes or rifles aimed on the prisoners are all elevated above them in guard stations or on the small ledge Captain Devol had the prisoners build halfway up two walls of the labor yard.

The captain waves one gloved hand at the gray dust surrounding him like a bad morning while the other clenches the thick black whip coiled on his hip. He walks the length of his ledge and shouts down at the powder-covered prisoners, "All right, slugs!"

All thirty-six men look up at him, each wearing a second skin of harsh powdered rock. Only their eyes betray the fact that they are humans underneath the layer of dust, and Captain Devol laughs at the irritated red eyes staring hatefully back at him. He tugs his pet whip from his hip and shakes it down at them. "I'm feeling chipper this fine summer eve. So I will give you slugs two minutes' rest before you gather yer stones and stack yer hammers and then drag yer sorry carcasses back in the pit!"

Every man amongst the thirty-six, save for one—Enos Bosworth—immediately sits down against the rock they have been beating for the past three hours. Groans and whimpers escape the men as their muscles shake and cramp from exhaustion. Men wipe the dust from their faces. Some cover their ears as if to silence the sound of metal chipping stone that echoes eternally in their eardrums, and a few steal glances of the treetops that surround the prison over the tall rock walls they've built. The thirty-six are all housed in the old shafts of the copper mine and are only allowed out of the dark, cold cells for their three to four hours of hard labor a day. Hard labor is still a new concept, an attempt at more humane punishment than lashes or stockades. But as Captain Devol proves, several who deal the punishment still prefer the flesh-searing lash and its immediate satisfaction to back-breaking work.

Enos never slows his pace as he stacks his last few hours' worth of rock chip. He never wipes the stinging dust from his face, and he never looks at the trees beyond the wall. Moses Lee sits with his back against a large granite slab, half tucked in the shade it provides and watches Enos.

"You can break for a minute, boy."

Enos doesn't break his stride but answers the older man. "I think the captain knows our muscles are burning and wanting to seize up on us. If we stop cold, they might not be able to move." He turns his head and eyes the thick black whip Captain Devol carries. "No matter for want."

"Fair enough, but is it really worse than when they take us back in the mine to our cells and our limbs fail us then? We all lie so still, pained, and useless as the bugs and rats crawl and chew at those same beaten muscles."

Enos finally pauses. He steps closer to Moses, leans to his ear, and whispers, "I like it down there."

"Bah!" Moses laughs. "No one likes it down there."

"I do. The dark and cool calm my angry spirit. Keep me from thieving."

"Bah!" Moses laughs again. "Keep up yer foolish talk and they'll drag ye to Hell's Hallway."

Enos's blue eyes light up, and he lowers his hammer and leans it against his leg. He wipes at the dust on his face, but his sweat has turned it to abrasive little balls that crumble between his fingers. He speaks in a clenched voice, whispering through a maniacal grin, "So only the mentally feeble live in Hell's Hallway?"

"Yeah." Moses stands, and his knees creak loudly while all his muscles scream silently. "Them, the Redcoats, and violent buggers. In fact, the last cell is a death sentence; none have survived their stay in it for long. Eldon Jackson cut himself up real bad about six months ago, and they been itching to fill it back up. It's not somewhere you wanna be, boy."

Enos is staring at Captain Devol talking to two other guards armed with rifles, but he answers Moses. "I do. My grandfather dug in Hellgate when it was Davenport Copper and Coal Company. He dug the last tunnel … the tunnel you call Hell's Hallway. My daddy gave me an old box that had a letter and a small chunk of stone. How do I get into that last cell?"

"Boy, you must be half foolish for wantin' to be anywhere near there, far removed from the deepest point in the mountain. That is crazy enough it just might do. Ask old Captain
Devol up there if he'd let you down there."

Moses scoffs into his hands.

Enos looks at the captain, and his eyes twitch involuntarily. He hates the captain. His flesh-searing whip. His brutal midnight visits. Enos swallows the hate rising in his throat, and it makes his stomach burn along with his muscles. He knows an easier way.

"Sorry, Moses," Enos mumbles as he raises his sledgehammer.

Moses tilts his head, a question on his lips, and Enos brings the eight-pound hammer down in the middle of the old man's forehead with enough force that his mouth relinquishes teeth instead of words. The end of the hammer cracks Moses's head open with a wet thwack that sounds like a parody of the former hammering sounds echoing in the ears of the men. Shards of skull fly, and blood spurts from the hammer's impact, which crumbles Moses's face and forehead to pulp.

The prisoners all shout and scream hoarsely even as they back away, fearing the hot musket balls destined to fly at Enos. Enos ignores both his fellow prisoners and the now-yelling guards, and he raises the gore-caked hammer again. The second blow hits the old man's head hard enough to tilt it in an unnatural direction with a stomach-turning crack. Enos hears the men behind howling at him, but a fresh fan of blood slaps across his face, and he ignores them still. He raises the hammer a third time and feels Captain Devol's whip cut through his tunic and tear a strip of flesh from his back. The crack the whip makes flinging his blood across the labor yard echoes over the screams and silences the men instantly.

Enos drops the hammer, but Captain Devol whips him twice more to ensure that his violence is done for now: once across his shoulder and once across the backs of his legs. Enos falls facefirst next to a faceless Moses, and

117

he stares through blurry eyes at the blood running off the old man's softly twitching hand to the dusty rock pile under him. The bright crimson of the blood stands out against the white of the dust and matches the pain Enos feels across his fresh wounds.

A black boot kicks Enos in the face, and he tries to curl into a ball. A second foot finds his spine, and he involuntarily unrolls and flops backwards into more angry black boots and gloved fists. The captain wraps the thick black leather of his whip around Enos's throat and drags him toward the open mouth of the former mine. Enos sees the dust-streaked faces of the other prisoners as he is dragged past them. He notices that some have hot red blood splattered across the dusty white. He smiles at them as he is pulled into the darkness.

### Main Labor Yard, Liberty Prison (formerly Hellgate Prison), Conn., Present

Owen Bosworth is growing impatient. He looks at the collapsing walls of the decaying prison around him and frowns. The walls begin as loosely stacked black rocks, and at the midway point, crudely fashioned red bricks complete the design. *Weak,* Owen thinks, *weak for a prison.* He knows nothing of the history of the centuries-old prison; he doesn't know or care that the walls were built by the prisoners themselves. He stares at the thick wooden doors that shut out the forest and keeps the ghosts of hundreds of men eternally imprisoned within the crumbling walls. Owen and his three-man team of attack lawyers are pacing the historic yard, awaiting the possible (though less likely by the second) arrival of a slew of oppositions to his newest plan to unearth a long-sealed mine shaft, in the form of city and state officials and rabid historical activists. Owen isn't worried. In fact, he is so confident that he has the excavating crew waiting down the road in their van for his phone call.

Owen Bosworth is rich enough that he can bully around officials of any rank. He can eat senators and congressmen and shit governors and mayors. A drive and desire for riches has been as strong a family trait as the thin hooked nose he proudly turns up at the common man. The Bosworths of his line have always been fueled by a never-ending greed, and they have possessed the ruthless power and cunning required to master such a trait and bend it to their satisfaction.

Owen is no exception. At thirty-nine, he is the youngest CEO ever of Bosworth Metals Inc., owner of three large mansions, each in a different country and climate, major stockholder in several important multi-national companies, and self-styled amateur treasure hunter. While going through bundles of family papers passed down from the time of the Revolutionary War, Owen stumbled across a hand-penned letter written from his great-great-great-uncle Enos Bosworth to his great-great-greatgrandfather John Bosworth.

*Dearest Brother John,*

*All I have endured has finally proved worthy. I sit now in the deepest darkest cell in Hellgate, the very same cell Grandfather wrote about. I have found the treasure he mentioned, and we will forever know riches and glory, dear brother. Enclosed is a small fragment of the rock that touches the coppery moss. See how it shines, dear brother, see the promises of wealth eternal in its sheen. I have chipped half the wall away and revealed a massive growth of the glowing moss; now commence your part of the plan. Get me and our glorious future out of this damned dark hole.*

*Your dear brother,*
*Enos Bosworth*
*Autumn, 1798*

Upon further study, Owen found that John Bosworth was, at the time, a well-respected lawyer in the small Connecticut town that housed the prison. John and Enos were never to meet back up, as the tunnel and cell about which Enos wrote were blasted closed soon after the letter was penned. The reason given in historical documents was that the shaft, then known as the ominous Hell's Hallway, was "found to be unsafe after the deaths of Enos Bosworth and several other prisoners, as well as two guards and their captain, James Devol."

Owen became obsessed with the letter and the mystery surrounding it. Pride roared and curiosity sang along with his ever-raging greed. If his great-uncle had found riches, even in the deep tunnels of a prison, then they were Bosworth riches. HIS riches. His mind raced and flashed vivid visions of him experiencing riches to dwarf those of any king of old. He bathed in the never-ending opulence, bedecked with rings with the teeth of his enemies stuck hard in gold and platinum, necklaces with leaves of pure ivory and silver, and robes with platinum-and-gold stitching. The vision faded slowly but remains forever in his mind.

Owen replays it now, behind his closed eyelids, as he waits for the rush of protest and camera crews behind the old wooden gate. He takes a deep breath of the warm Connecticut breeze. He holds the breath, allows himself to taste the earth and the trees, before releasing it. He exhales moist air. He inhales again and tastes gold and copper. He holds the breath, tastes the blood and dirt, before swallowing it into his chest.

With his eyes still closed and mind still seeing himself in flowing robes, walking along a river of blood that runs through his harem, he asks the lawyers, "What time is it?"

All three look at their Rolex watches and answer in unison, "One minute to eleven."

A pickup skids to a stop outside the closed gate. Owen's eyes remain closed, but his lips worm into a smile.

The door to the vehicle slams, and the wide wooden gate is pushed open. A single man in faded blue coveralls bearing a patch that says "Buck" and wearing a scowl and a frown under his black handlebar mustache marches past them to the entrance of the mine.

"So, a whole lotta good men woke up this morning to more pressing matters than some rich asshole blasting apart something with God damned historical value," the old groundskeeper nearly shouts at the four men. Owen reaches for his phone with his eyes still closed, and thumbs a button to connect him to the team down the road.

"Seems a coupla videos got sent to the proper places to get a few fellas in heaps of trouble. They can't afford to fight ya any more."

Owen's three lawyers are powerful and dangerous monsters themselves. He knows at least one man has swallowed a handgun this morning during an impromptu meeting with his lawyers. Wait until Buck hears his favorite congressman would rather put his brains on the wall behind him than have people find out he wears women's underwear and chokes himself during sex. Rabid activists were tamed when their loudest voice, MaryJane Honeyworth, was found to really be Victoria Eldrod, the youngest and last captured member of the infamous Church of the Black Goat cult from the late seventies. Owen knows no one will want to support any cause once hailed by a member of the infant-sacrificing cult. Buck, as furious as he may be, is the quiet submission of all in his path. Open the door, and the bad man will stop. At least they hope.

"We're ready," he speaks into his phone.

"You are a son of a bitch," Buck says inches from Owen's closed eyes.

Owen hears him. Richardson, the oldest and most ruthless of Owen's team, answers the old man. "Open the door, Buck. You can't afford any trouble."

"Well, you greasy shit stain, I ain't got shit fer money, so I could kick all yer asses, and you can't take shit from me! Ha!"

The old man nods his head crazily at the four men in turn. Owen's eyes are still shut tight, and the lawyers' eyes all bore slow, cold holes into Buck. He steps back and spits at Owen's feet.

"Answer me, you son of a bitch!"

Owen ignores him, and Richardson answers. "So, we'll see how your sister and brother-in-law, Beth and Todd, like it when they have to explain to your little niece, Melissa, that her scholarship to college has been revoked."

Richardson pauses and smirks when Buck winces at the names of his beloved family. Owen hears the wince like a scream and the smirk like a guffaw.

"Or your uncle Jed in Falterwood Assisted Living might just find himself cold, lonely, and most certainly senile, wandering the streets in a faraway Idaho town. So swing away." Owen smiles and knows his lawyers are smiling too, all without opening his eyes. He hears Buck's will break as the proud working0class man realizes he is up against a truly wicked rival. The old groundskeeper doesn't even grumble as he unlocks the master lock on the door to the dangerous ancient mine shafts. He sighs once and turns away, wordless. Buck stares at the ground as he walks past the blasting crew as they trot to their job.

With the door finally open, Owen opens his eyes and steps into the darkness of the mine with a smile.

### Underground Prison Cells (Hell's Hallway), Hellgate Prison, Conn., 1798

As Enos disappears into the mouth of the dark hallway that leads to the former mine, the prisoners outside wake from their shocked stupor and begin screaming. Even with Devol's whip wrapped so tight that the leather digs into his neck, Enos laughs. A few cracks of gunfire calm the prisoners outside, but not the kicking Enos. Captain Devol pulls him backwards to the staircase and drops him hard on his back. The two guards accompanying Devol immediately start kicking Enos in his chest and ribs.

The smoke from the torches that light the underground cavern fills the stale air and stings Enos's eyes. He gets one last glimpse at the dwindling entranceway before Devol tugs him backwards down the stairs with a series of thumps and crashes. Once at the bottom of the stairs, the guards kick and stomp again.

Devol curses and spits at Enos as he drags him deeper and deeper into the underground prison by his neck. Enos gags and chokes and laughs when he manages a breath.

The four work their way to the deepest cells in the prison, the aptly named Hell's Hallway, the same way. Devol is dragging, cursing, and spitting; Enos is gagging, laughing, and kicking weakly. The two guards stomp and kick whenever Devol pauses long enough to give them the chance.

By the time they reach Enos's new cell, the very deepest cell in the mountain, he can't feel his legs, and both his eyes are swollen shut. Devol drags Enos into the darkness, and he yells at the other two guards to leave them. They wait and watch their captain unwrap his whip from Enos's throat, but they don't move.

He turns at them, fury dancing in his eyes and flickering from the nearby torchlight. "I said leave us be!"

The two guards mumble apologies and fall over each other fleeing their boss. Devol tugs at his belt and kicks a stilllaughing Enos in his ribs. Enos curls up in a ball and spits blood across the black stone floor of his new cell. From across the small hallway, a voice steals Devol's attention.

"Here I don't even get visitors, and this chap gets the full Colonial welcome from you, Captain Devol."

Devol frowns and cracks his whip from inside Enos's cell. Enos curls even tighter on the floor, his wounds screaming in response to the sound of the weapon splitting the air above him. The vicious end of the whip cuts across the fingers of the talking man wrapped around his cell bars. He howls, pulls his bleeding hand to his chest, and backs quickly into the darkness of his cell.

From the mouth of the mine prison, the sound of musket fire rings dully down to them. Screams and yells accompany the gunshots, some muffling them, others embellishing the loud popping sounds echoing down through the tunnels. The prisoners outside might be rioting.

Devol leans down and grabs Enos by the back of his head with a handful of dirty blond hair. "I'll be back. For every prisoner killed because of your madness out there, I'll give you ten lashes." Warm spittle splatters Enos's bloody, swollen face, burning the numerous cuts and scrapes, as Devol leans even closer. "For every guard I lose, I'll give you twenty and a good buggering."

Enos groans weakly in response. Devol slams Enos's head against the stone floor and stands to face the other prisoner.

"I'll be back for you too, mate."

"I look forward to it, Captain."

Devol grunts and walks back up toward the sounds of chaos above. He pauses, grabs the torch from the earth wall and, with a smile, drops it into the bucket of shit and piss the men share. The torch sizzles and goes out. Darkness swallows the two prisoners in their cells.

Enos chuckles a few times, wet hacking sounds, while he rolls around the cold floor of his new cell. The torch Devol extinguished was the only one for the small, oddly shaped cell block. Around a small bow in the rock that creases a corner into the walkway and up a few unevenly sized stairs, a row of torches light a more conventional cell block. The glow from those torches tickles and teases at the small corner, but leaves Enos and the other man in darkness.

The prisoner across the narrow hallway calls to him from the blackness. "Hard to believe, but that son of a bitch Captain Devol did us a favor by dousing our torch in shit."

"You have a kind and patient cullyman down here?" Enos gags. "A man so wretched he doesn't mind digging a torch from our shit just so we can fill the bucket and he can carry it up top?"

"No," the man and the voice creep closer to Enos. "But without the torchlight, you can't see what I gotta warn you about. You have a better chance than most of avoiding it and its madness because of this smelly darkness."

Enos strains and curses but manages to sit up. "Does the new cell come with a nest of nasty spiders *and* a talkative new neighbor?"

He laughs out loud, the pain in his ribs a searing throb that threatens to loosen his urinary tract.

"I'm going to tell you, whether you are coherent or worthy of my advice," the voice sighs, hidden back in the darkness, "for *my* piece of mind."

Enos struggles, each tiny movement a painful battle and monumental victory, to reach into his pocket. He manages a short chuckle when his fingers find the small chip of stone, but it costs him a mouthful of warm blood. He smiles wide, and blood trickles thickly down his chin to his ripped and filthy tunic as he crawls to the far wall of his tiny cell.

The voice in the darkness continues. "I've been here for, I think, two years. I'm a prisoner of war, though they won't admit it. I'm still waiting to see a so-called judge. It's hard to judge time when you never leave your cell. Even harder still when your cell is deep in a mountainside, like the one in which I currently reside."

Curiosity momentarily distracts Enos from his maniacal greed and, though he still struggles to feel the wall with both hands, he says, "Go on, then."

The voice in the dark, obviously excited to have someone to listen to him, inches closer. Enos hears the man grip the bars as he had before Captain Devol whipped his knuckles. Enos runs his hands over the cell wall in the dark; he feels how cold and smooth the wall is in spots and how jagged and sharp it is in others. He holds the small rock chip from his grandpa's letter between two fingers on his right hand, and it scrapes softly against the surface as he searches for where it fits.

"There is something in that cell that makes men lose their minds, mate. I know how preposterous that sounds, but I've watched five men go insane in the time I've been here. Rascals and idiots all, but something in that cell twisted their simple minds and made them dangerous."

The man pauses as if to gauge Enos's interest. Enos says nothing, but his breath comes in wet ragged bursts, and the sound echoes through the small cell block a few times before the voice speaks again. "There is something, a scratch or a chip, on the wall near the corner. I warn you so you don't look, mate."

Enos swallows a painful lump in his throat and water drips from his swollen eyes. He hopes that when he speaks, he doesn't sound overexcited. "What is this *thing?*"

"I'm not sure, as I can't see it from my cell. A few of the men have tried to describe it to me as it chewed away at their sanity. The best and most common description is a strange glowing moss that peeks out from the chip in the wall. The more the men stare at it, the more greed consumes them. Even as they grow more insane with thoughts of treasure and glory, the fact that they are stuck down here to rot triggers a violent reaction. Three have died by their own hands, two I stood and watched screaming for help as they cut themselves to ribbons. The other two were killed by the guards when they finally

129

slipped off the boat of sanity and into the sea of violence. Both of those I saw. Screaming didn't help then either."

"A moss," Enos chokes, "a shimmering moss that plays with the minds of men? Have you been here for so long you've nothing better to do than speak such things?"

"John Mallard," the voice in the darkness says slightly louder, so it resonates against the walls, "was the first. He earned his prison sentence for stealing horses, and he earned your cell for stabbing a guard in the neck. He told me he could see 'riches beyond comprehension' shimmering at him from the crack in the wall. Within a week, all he did was stand, swaying and drooling, and stare at the moss in the wall."

"Sounds terrible," Enos grumbles.

"It wasn't so bad. At least until I woke one morning to the cullyman vomiting in the hallway. I could never hold a fit of sickness against a cullyman, but he was weeping like a child, and *that* drew my attention. I stood and noticed blood running into my cell from yours."

The man in the darkness across from Enos kneels in his cell, cursing his wounded fingers as he rifles though a small chest. He retrieves something from the chest and taps something metal on his cell bars.

"This same floor," the voice says, and Enos hears a small coin roll from the stranger's cell to his. Even with his eyes swollen shut, Enos leans away from his search of the walls and towards the rolling coin. As soon as he does, he realizes the uphill slant to the stranger's cell. Enos catches the coin and taps it on the floor.

"I crept slowly to my cell bars and the heaving man just beyond them. He was on his hands and knees in a thick puddle of John Mallard. All that was left of John Mallard was a puddle of gore on the floor.

"The man after him was named William Bloom. He killed the captain of the guards before lovely old Devol. A musket ball to his forehead ended his madness. After him, was Richard Clayman. Mr. Clayman told me all the riches in the world awaited him.
Only it would cost him his flesh."

"A pound of flesh," Enos croaks.

The voice ignores the interruption completely, as if the man is lost in memories. "I watched him stab a fork into his arm until it tore a big enough hole that he could rip his skin away. I stood and screamed for a guard while he peeled his arm, then his chest. He skinned both of his arms and legs, his chest and belly, and most of his face before he fell dead in the middle of the cell.
His blood ran into my cell as well."

Enos taps the coin on the floor in response.

"Joseph Collins earned the cell next after raping a young housemaid. He only lasted three days. I watched him stand drooling and swaying for most of those three days. When he did move, he dove at a guard and ripped his throat asunder with his teeth. A whistle to wake the dead screamed through the caverns, and every guard was on him. They beat him past a pulp. Just ... to nothing."

Enos knows the story from here. "And old Moses Lee told me, right before I caved his skull in, that Eldon Jackson went an' cut himself up real bad. And here we are."

Enos turns back to his search for the chip's home in the wall without another word.

"I told you what I had to tell you. Think what you will, take my words as you will, but I've said my piece. What happens now is at your discretion. I'm being honest, no matter how it sounds, and that makes my soul feel at ease for once. Allow that pound to be the only riches you dream of, mate."

Enos wants to scoff at the man, but as the chip in his hand slips into place in the wall above him with a tiny "clink," his mind swirls with thoughts of gold temples and rivers of blood, and his scoff dies in his pained throat.

### Underground Prison Cells, Liberty Prison (formerly Hellgate Prison), Conn., Present

Owen walks into the mouth of the underground prison, and his eyes adjust quickly to the dim light cast by a string of wire-covered bulbs that line the wall. He smiles at his lawyers, and they smile back, a circle of sharks and demons grinning like gleeful villains. Baker, his lawyer in

132

the blue power suit, greets the blasting-crew foreman. The foreman and Baker compare identical shaft maps, and the foreman, a stalky, pale-faced man with a company polo shirt on, motions to his crew. Half a dozen men rush by Owen and his lawyers, each with arms full of equipment.

Jones, the third of Owen's lawyers, sporting a light gray Armani suit, is handed earplugs, clear protective goggles, and four white hardhats from the last crewman. Jones distributes them to the other three elegantly dressed men standing in the mouth of an ex-mine/prison.

"How long until they begin blasting?" Owen is excited, and it sounds like a whine when he asks.

Baker, Jones, and Richardson all look at each other, none really knowing the answer.

Owen only endures a split second of silence before he sighs disappointedly.

Richardson opens his mouth to say something, but someone grabs him from behind and puts the muzzle of a Desert Eagle .45 to the side of his head before a word can escape. Owen smiles and takes a small step back, as do Jones and Baker. Richardson raises his hands slowly without being asked to by the assailant still hiding behind him.

Owen smiles and sees golden walls over the cold, dark stone like a dream. He smells blood. Richardson sees the smile on his employer's face and misreads it, thinking it one of extreme confidence. Richardson assumes Buck went to his pickup, grabbed some steel manhood, and is seeking retribution for his legal threats.

"Boy, did I rub you the wrong way there, Buck?" Richardson still has a smile on his face. He still thinks the weak, broken, easy-to-manipulate Buck is behind him. It's his last thought as a bullet tears his brains through a fist-sized crater in the side of his head. His eyes bulge and bleed as he falls forward. Owen and his remaining two lawyers take more steps back, closer to the staircase.

A short woman with waist-length auburn hair stands where Richardson had moments before. A splash of clumpy maroon crosses her face, giving her the look of a warrior. She points the gun at Jones with a sure and steady hand.

She asks the three men, "Do you know who I am?"

Owen shakes his head "no." He looks at Jones and Baker, both of whom are staring at the woman wearing a bandolier of cartridges for the weapon in her small hand and a ragged sundress.

She kicks Richardson's twitching corpse and lines up the barrel with Jones's nose.

"I'm not gonna ask again."

Both Jones and Baker reluctantly nod "yes."

"Good. Then you know you've ruined the life I've built for myself. You know I ..."

Owen's impatience and self-importance flare twin fires of insult, and he steps forward. "I don't know who you are, so introductions would still be considered polite."

"Oh, I'm important enough for you to destroy, but not important enough to ever gaze upon." The madness of her words matches a growing glow in her eyes. "I'm Victoria Eldrod. Last living or free member of the Church of the Black Goat. But until last night, I had a new name. A new life." she chokes back tears. "And you are every bit as evil as the high priests of *that cult*."

She spits the last and levels the gun at Owen. He blinks once, full of confidence.

Tears blur her vision, and she lowers the gun a little. "Evil men want down that tunnel. The Church of the Black Goat was sacrificing infants to ancient dark gods in hopes to unearth the tunnel you are planning on blasting open this morning. I can't allow whatever is down there out. I've dedicated my life to keeping people out and away. I've done everything I could do to repent. I knew this was coming."

Two tears roll down each of her flushed red cheeks, and she brings the gun level with Owen's face again. "I didn't know the federal agents would raid my house with live guns. I *had* a husband and two children. Here, I come to find out, men are still sacrificing children to this tunnel. My own children's blood was spilled in the quest for that tunnel. No more."

135

She waves the men toward the stairs with the Desert Eagle. The three men all look at each other. The smell of Richardson's body expelling all its waste hurries their decision not to argue with Victoria Eldrod. They lead the way down the stone stairs. None of them is smiling.

### Enos Bosworth's Cell on Hell's Hallway, Hellgate Prison, Conn., 1799

Enos hears James screaming, but he doesn't care what he is saying. Enos saw the moss. He saw it shimmer and wave. He saw vivid visions of wealth almost laughable in its excess. The desire for the reality of the vision consumed his mind. Unlike the others before him, Enos has been affected from birth. When his grandfather chipped the stone away, the instant before the announcement of the immediate addition of criminals to do the back-breaking labor of mining, the moss sank its tendrils of hunger and death in. Its madness ran through their blood.

Enos watches the shimmering moss as he chips away at the wall around it. He feels it is pleased at being exposed to more and more air. The moss has been in the mountainside for centuries. When it arrived on this planet, it was but a tiny vicious spore. It sank into the mountain and has been growing ever since, pulsing and glowing as it twists the minds of every human to gaze upon it. It knows only desire and chaos. It spreads only greed and death.

The moss has no name, though the Church of the Black Goat called it Grave Mold. The moss calls to the wicked men around it with dreams and visions it sends through solid stone walls. The evil men are left with an impression more than a true vision of what sends them the dreams. In reality, it is an ancient and terrible cosmic parasite, nameless and thoughtless, that exists only to propagate itself and destroy the world around it.

Enos raises his small work hammer and chips more rock away from the wall. At first only a few tiny pebbles fall, but then, with a terribly loud crunch, a third of Enos's wall crumbles to his cell floor. Dust and pebbles fill the hallway, and the other three men in the small cell block all shield their eyes. Enos smiles at the wall's collapse, glad he sent his brother the letter telling him he was done here. Suddenly, he doesn't want to leave. The moss is glowing so bright the weak flickering torch in the hall seems pale and useless. The light from the moss blinds James Goodchild, the man who warned Enos of the moss from the shadows his first night.

James shields his eyes and screams for guards and help. The two other prisoners soak up his fear, both unable to tell where the sudden and malevolent light shines from, and they scream as well. Relief flushes James Goodchild as he hears the pounding of boots running his direction from the caverns above, but still he screams.

Enos waves the dust away from his vision and stands in front of a glowing, pulsing wall. He sees more riches than entire worlds would need at his feet. He feels the power. He feels greed and desire.

The moss glimmers and shines a darker gold for but an instant, and suddenly Enos understands the cost of all the riches his mind can dream. The riches aren't for the beings of the flesh; they are too vast and too valuable. Only a man with skin of moss could possess such riches. Enos reaches his hand up to the jagged break in the wall and drags it across it quickly, sending a thin fan of blood across his face. He smiles when the trick works and tears a wicked gash on his hand. He digs two fingers into the wound and grabs the skin hard. James is still yelling, but it sounds like a dream. Enos tugs and pulls a flap of skin away from his wrist and toward his stiff fingers. James screams and screams, muffled like he is underwater. Enos tugs again. And again.

Captain Devol storms into the cell block, flanked by two guards and cracking his whip as he rounds the corner. The first two prisoners cower at the sight of Devol, but James screams hoarsely and points to Enos's cell.

Devol shields his eyes from the bright glow and inches forward, barking threats as he moves. "Bosworth, I pray you have set yourself on fire. I do not intend to deal with another mess from that cursed cell. I'll flail the flesh from your back for this one."

Enos hears the captain as he hears James, muffled and distant. He has pulled all the skin off his hand and is holding the twitching meat of his skinless hand inches from the moss. Captain Devol strides to Enos's cell at the exact instant the glowing moss reaches a tiny fuzzy finger to Enos's bloody paw. It tickles the exposed muscle a few quick times before wrapping around it. In a flash, the moss splits. The moss on the wall glimmers a brilliant flash of bright sunshine gold. The moss on Enos's hand wraps tight and spreads quickly, eating away at muscle and flesh, blood and bone as it goes.

Enos raises his hand and stares dumbly at the golden moss pulsing and growing there. He turns and shows Devol his moss-covered hand. The captain scowls and watches the loose shape of Enos's hand shift into a bulbous, lopsided form without any fingers. Blood runs in thick streams from Enos's hand down his elbow and to the stone floor below him. The blood flees uphill toward Captain Devol and James Goodchild. Devol is completely entranced with Enos and his flesh-eating moss, watching the glow of satisfied madness in his eyes, and then the stump of his hand shifts again and is far smaller, perhaps having been consumed past the wrist.

The two other guards clamor close to Devol, successfully blocking James's view of the carnage. He screams at them but is ignored. He slams his hands on the cell bars, but he is again ignored. His throat burns from yelling, and his chest hurts from his intense panic. He gives up yelling and pounding on the bars.

James realizes every muscle in his body is rigid with fear, and he tries to relax. He puts his hands on his knees, closes his eyes, and takes a deep breath. He opens his eyes and sees a creek of blood flowing into his cell. His wide eyes look to the backs of the guards, fully blocking Enos's cell but not the shimmering light cast by the moss.

He reaches quickly through his cell bars and pulls the sidearm from each of the two guards. He cocks both hammers, and the loud clacks distract Devol and his weaponless guards. They turn to face the man who is pointing guns at them. James sees Enos behind them, his arm gone and moss creeping across his chest, down his legs, and up his neck.

The moss on the wall shimmers the darker shade of gold, just for an instant. James pulls one trigger. Enos's head snaps back with a smoking black hole in the center, and he stumbles, but he doesn't fall. The gunshot wakes everyone in the cell block from their trances. Devol bellows and charges James's cell, slamming against the steel bars as he fights to open it. James raises the second pistol and gives Devol a smoking hole to match Enos's.

The captain stumbles backwards into Enos's cell bars with a clatter. The two guards panic, staring back and forth at James and Captain Devol. James drops both pistols, useless now without more ammunition.

Devol croaks something unintelligible, and all the men look at him.

Enos slams into the bars, now barely recognizable as human. He is covered in the glowing moss, and as he leans toward them, his human shape falls away under the pulsing golden moss only to roll and twist into new odd shapes and bumps. A mossy arm reaches up around Devol's gaping mouth, and small tendrils of glimmering moss dance in his mouth and up his nose. In seconds, bright golden moss sprouts from the dark hole in Devol's forehead. Then it sprouts from his ears, and his eyes cover over in a mossy sheen.

One guard bolts out of the glowing hallway. The other waits but a second too long, and Devol's dead hand reaches up with inhuman speed. The guard gags and kicks against the dead man's iron grip as James moves to the very back of his cell. His throat hurts too much to scream for help anymore. He stares at the writhing guard on the floor, watching as glowing moss covers the fist gripped on his windpipe. It spreads to the guard's face as if it were the exact same skin as the hand choking it. In less than a minute, both men are covered by the glowing moss. Their shapes fall away and roll into different shapes as they move.

The thing that used to be Devol never lets go of the thing that used to be the guard. Both mossy creatures stand and shuffle in opposite directions. The guard-thing leans in toward James, and the Devol-thing leans to the next cell, where it claps onto a hand clenched white-knuckle tight on the bars. As the guardthing lunges at James, he notices the Enos-thing still connected with the Devol-thing through the bars. The mossy guard-thing leans its head against the bars of James's cell. The glowing moss shimmers as it quickly covers the cold steel.

James hears the footfalls of more guards and leans forward to scream that he is alive. The moss reaches a hand from the bars and claps tight on his mouth. Moss spreads over his lips and nose in an instant. His eyes tear up and shiver as he hears the unmistakable sizzle of dynamite. Golden moss covers his vision as the doorway to the cell block is blasted shut.

Under the golden moss, everything looks red.

### *Former Entrance to Hell's Hallway, Liberty Prison (Formerly* Hellgate Prison), Conn., Present

Owen smiles confidently in the dim glow of the wirecovered bulbs, even though Victoria Eldrod has the business end of a .45 nestled behind his ear like a cold steel lover. He feels the gun barrel, and every time it tickles his skin, he remembers the puff of smoke that spat from it and through Richardson's skull. It rubs death on him with steel kisses. It won't delay him for long. Even as they walk the twisting tunnels, he sees golden walls instead of the scuffed worn black the others see. Owen feels the riches pulsing and calling to him. A tiny little gun isn't going to stop him.

As the four of them start down the last small incline to the former entrance, four shadows dart across the far end of the tunnel. Victoria slams Owen into the wall and shouts at Jones and Baker to get down and then at the fleeing men to halt. Her voice echoes through the stone corridor but the shadows vanish quickly, and the sound of hurried footfalls above them brings a harsh laugh from Owen.

His face pushed against the cool stone, Owen says, "The workers are set to blow the opening. They'll be up above ground within a minute, and you'd better believe they heard your gunshot and will call the cops."

Victoria pushes the gun barrel into the tender flesh of Owen's neck as she answers, "I followed them through the gate. There were six of them. That leaves two still down here."

She pulls on the back of Owen's shirt. He winces as he hears the tiny unmistakable tear of his ultra-fine shirt. Owen leans away from the wall and scowls at the frightened look he sees in Baker's eyes. Jones is looking down the darkest, smallest hallway yet. Victoria nudges Owen forward, and the lawyers lead them all deeper.

Jones and Baker come into view of the foreman and a second worker, a skinny kid of about twenty two or so, with their hands held up.

"Jesus Christ," the foreman stammers, "we heard gunshots, is everything ..."

He stops mid-sentence when Owen is pushed into the corner of stone lined with fine blasting wires. Victoria turns her hand cannon on the foreman and his worker.

143

Both jump away from the gun and hold their hands up as well. A crooked smile crosses Victoria's face, and she motions to the two workers to stand by the others. They shuffle to comply with the unspoken order.

"Tell them to pack it up and go home," she orders Owen with the .45 at his eye level.

"Are we all ready to blast?"

Every eye in the darkened cavern goes wide at Owen's question. His eyes scan the wall and the tiny multicolored wires that criss-cross it. The corners of his mouth curl up in a wicked and satisfied grin. He feels his destiny pulsing behind the wall.

Almost on instinct alone, the foreman answers dumbly, "yes, sir, all set."

Victoria shakes her head, as if to awaken from a crazy dream where she's lost control, even with the big gun. She jabs Owen in the neck with the gun. She feels the pattern of the grip dig into the soft flesh of her palm. It isn't enough to get Owen's attention. She quickly turns the gun on Jones and pulls the trigger. Jones attempts to duck, but the bullet rips through the chest of his blue suit, trailing acrid smoke. Blood spatters the wall behind him as he tips forward, lifeless. Baker looks back the way they just came, preparing to make a break for it.

A bullet hits him in the temple, foiling his plan, as bullet tears through brain. He gurgles something and stumbles into the corner, his skull spilt wide open and leaking gray matter down his blank face. He leans against the wall and slides slowly down it. Once he reaches the ground, his head rolls to the side, still looking back the way they came, so Owen can have a good view of his blasted-open head.

The kid next to the foreman tries to run past the carnage, shoving Owen aside as he goes. Victoria yells for him to stop, but he takes two more long, quick steps before two bullets pierce his skinny back and drop him, twitching and screaming, to the floor.

She turns back to the foreman and tells him, sadly and honestly, "I don't want to kill you, but I will. This man is evil. Whatever is behind this wall is evil. I can't allow it to be free. I know you don't understand, but I won't let this happen."

Owen, unfazed by the brutal deaths of his attorneys three is leaning against the wall, feeling power and wealth pulse against him. He closes his eyes and sees his golden temple. He sees the river of blood flowing in front of him. In his eyes, he is leaning on the wall of his temple, rumples in his flowing robes. Victoria is standing next to the river of blood floating through Owen's vision. The foreman is standing in front of an even more elaborately carved golden wall, his hands in the air, begging mercy.

Owen hears Victoria's voice, distant and muffled even though she is only a few feet from him. The wall vibrates softly and he springs forward, slamming her into the wall face-first. She screams as Owen bounces her skull repeatedly into the unforgiving stone. Blood soaks her long hair, and Owen wraps her bloody locks around his tightly clenched fist for a better grip. The Desert Eagle slips from her twitching hand, and Owen stops banging her head against the wall. He stands to face the foreman, then decides to pick up the gun.

He turns to the foreman, still standing frozen and watching everything, and notices a wet spot covering the front of the man's jeans. The foreman's hands are still up. In his left hand, Owen sees a small piece of plastic with an illuminated digital face.

"Is that the detonator?" Owen asks, pointing at the thing in his hand.

"Yeah," is all the man can manage to say, unable to tear his eyes away from the three dead men and the seriously injured woman strewn about the crowded hallway.

"Okay," Owen says, the confident smile returning to his sweaty face. "Help me move her."

Owen grabs Victoria under her arms and drags her across the floor. She moans as she moves, and blood runs in a steady stream from a wound hidden under her hair. He drags her to the corner, her feet trailing weakly behind, and heaves her at Jones's corpse. She lands on the lifeless body, moaning and struggling weakly. Owen pushes her hair out of her face, tucking it behind her ear, and wipes blood off her cheek.

"Where do we need to stand while you blow this?"

The foreman looks at Owen and shakes his head frantically. "I can't blow it now. I have to call the cops."

"I'm the boss, and I say blow it!"

"I can't, Mr. Bosworth; it's murder."

Owen sighs indignantly and waves his hands at the mass of bodies, "Even after watching her kill my attorneys? And your worker?"

The foreman shakes his head again and walks toward the door. "I can't. I just can't, Mr. Bosworth."

"Fine," Owen says and waves his hand at the foreman, dismissing him.

The foreman turns to leave, and Owen raises the gun and puts a slug through the fleeing man's head. The foreman stumbles forward, the top half of his head missing, and falls on his dead employee. Owen simply walks up and pulls the remote from the dead man's hand. He glances back at the wall. Victoria Eldrod is lying between the bodies of Jones and Baker, crying, moaning, and trying in vain to stand. Owen scoffs at her and walks around the small corner and up the small incline into the hallway above. He leans against the far wall, shields his face from any debris, and pushes the button on the remote.

The blast is immediate and fierce, sending a plume of rock-filled dust up past a cowering Owen with enough force to shatter most of the lights strung the length of the wall. The entire mountain moans like the dead, and the lights not destroyed by the blast flicker weakly. Owen waits, sheltered against the wall, for the dust to clear. When it does, he walks proudly down the incline and back into the small dark hallway.

Owen hears sirens far above. As he rounds the corner, the sound of them fades and buzzes into nothingness. The wall has been successfully destroyed, leaving only dirty wet stains where five corpses had been piled. Owen steps over the chunks of rock not turned to powder by the explosion and looks down Hell's Hallway.

A glimmering gold moss coats the walls and floors of the ancient hallway, beckoning Owen into it. The moss shimmers and shines, casting a gruesome glow across Owen's face. He sees the golden walls of the temple in his visions. He is home.

Owen steps over the carnage and through the doorway to
claim his boundless treasures.

# MC STITCHES

*"Mic check one, two, one, two."*

And then the screaming starts. No one hears it but MC
Stitches.

He sits in his basement cage, composing the dopest beats humankind has ever dared to imagine. Deep vibrating organ pipes thicken the rapid, pulsing drum 'n' bass, adding an element of malevolence and a layer of pure funky groove. Then the first looped scream repeats. The howl of pain is intimate and pure. It is his scream from when he carved out his right eye for its stubborn refusal to look toward the future. It churns an avalanche of regret within his bowels, and he smashes his forehead against the cage to retain the focus needed for his opus.

Blood drizzles down from the fresh gash and makes crimson lightning streaks across the oversized lens of his goggles. With one two-fingered hand, he cues up the next scream. With his other hand, frighteningly complete with all five spindly fingers, he turns a knob and stretches the beats beyond the intro. The scream set to join the loop 'n' groove, he reaches his two twitchy digits and flips the switch to the three hanging 17-inch black-light tubes attached to the roof of his cage.

The flood of dark light illuminates the crowd of five corpses littered around his basement stage. The second scream, the first he ever stole, falls into groove after his shriek amidst the pounding rhythm. His audience sits motionless, tied to chairs with duct tape and barbed wire. Their mouths hang open, eyeless sockets swallowing the light and drooling it down pale scarred cheeks. The cherry veins across his goggles glow a deep, romantic red, and his remaining eye tears. Two fingers give the spinning record a quick scratch, then cue the next pair of screams. One deep and one shrill, they capture and rape the high and low ends of the ever-evolving groove in an aural masterpiece. Only MC
Stitches hears it.

He grabs the mic with his complete hand and shouts through his spittle-soaked bandana in his broken voice.

*"Everybody get up!"*

Though his bastardized soundboards could easily replicate and repeat the phrase, he shouts a slightly less rowdy echo.

*"Get up! Get up!"*

None of his corpse groupies moves, but their lack of devotion to the groove doesn't deter him any. They each had chances to listen to his epic song. Extraordinary, unbelievably kind glimpses into his terrible towering masterpiece he offered them. Each cowered in fear. Each refused to see the beauty, dark and ferocious, in the gift of groove he offered them. So he added them to the mix. Each was good for at least a scream or two, a sobbing whine, or a gurgled whimper. Each became a part of the groove. Only MC Stitch hears them.

His head bobs constantly, the groove ringing and throbbing in his ears and soul. He is a constant blur as the song builds and falls back on itself. Within a few minutes, there are so many screams looping that they run end to end, rendering the groove, so tight and so dope, utter chaos. Sweat mingles with the blood drizzling down his face, giving him an iodine-colored sheen in the black light. At the thirteen-minute mark, MC Stitches feels his epic taking shape.

*"Can you dig it? Dig it! Dig it!"* he screams hoarsely into the mic. Then he reaches his good hand into the blades of the industrial fan perched on his cage to cool him and keep the reek of the corpses away from him.

The fingers don't cut cleanly, but rather break and tear away from his pointy knuckles, giving the powerful blades something to choke on. He screams, he knows he does because it scratches his dry throat, yet he doesn't hear it. He has confidence he managed to record it. The fan blades stutter against bone, and the motor grinds in response. He pulls his hand away, and the blades resume full speed and fling blood and pulp across the crowded basement. MC Stitches waves his fresh stump in the air like he just don't care.

He uses his two fingers—his only fingers now—to play back the sound of his groove-sacrificed self-mutilation. Louder, slurred like a drunk, and overlapped by looping screams. He feels it. He reaches up and tugs the bandana from his face. With his two-fingered talon, he brings the microphone to his lipless face.

A shout from above interrupts him.

"Gordon!"

The groove is ruined. Thudding bass is creaking into quick silence, the screams weakening into chuckles. Yet the echo of his living-ghost father's baritone haunts still.

"Ribs could be broken!"

MC Stitches digs his fingers into his lacerated hand and rocks back and forth. His father isn't upstairs. His father is a windborne demon, forever slipping in, out, gone.

"Everything you do is failure except hurt, boy!"

Two blood-streaked fingers tug one plug from an outlet in the wall and plug in another hanging nearby. Black light blinks off. A string of 50-watt bulbs ooze on, flooding the room with a dismal glow. It the split second of transition, MC Stitches sees the roomful of corpses sigh. He'd kill them again if he could. He'd enjoy it, because the first time, every bruise, every cut, every scream was for the groove. And their squeals and grunts and wails of pain still weren't enough for his epic. He sulks past his rotting captive audience and up the rotting wooden stairs, knowing it needs something more. One more scream, caught from a confrontation that dwells in memories and nightmares, a scream from a windborne demon. Only MC Stitches hears it.

# AMPUTEE DISCO AND THE LORD OF THE GROOVE

I was hanging by my neck when I first saw the lights from the Amputee Disco through the tall evergreens. I strung myself up with a length of neon cord I found in a decrepit shack. Two demons perched on the branch above me, and a blue jay stood on the knot of neon cord tied there. I swung content, the noose around my neck tight enough to keep me from choking up my sins. The demons grew bored with my lack of kicking and twitching and began tickling me. Tickles feel different to everyone. It wasn't entirely unpleasant. However, it wasn't entirely pleasing either. A hug for an enemy, a betrayal for a friend.

"What are those lights?" I gagged around neon cord.

The demons, tired of tickling me and of my kicking and twitching, flapped back to the branch above me.

"That's the Amputee Disco," they answered in eerie unison.

I gagged as gravity tugged at my feet.

"Are you trying to tell me you'd rather dance than death dangle?" the blue jay asked me.

I gagged on the bright pink froth foaming from my mouth.

"Might as well," the demons spoke together. "At the Amputee Disco, one is cellmate with the other."

They reached together and nipped the neon cord with their claws. The knot unraveled quickly, and smoke rose from the branch as it whipped toward freedom. I fell toward the forest floor, where I crashed in a heap. I landed on my pinkie. The poor little digit broke quite severely, and pinkie bone poked through pinkie flesh.

"You had that coming," the demons hollered down at me.

"I may well have," I shouted back up at them. "Thank you for your judgment."

"Think nothing of it!" they shouted back. "You owe us, fucker!"

The blue jay held a scrap of paper in its beak. I tilted my head like a questioning dog, and the blue jay opened its beak, dropping the paper. It flittered on the breeze, floating down to me like the ash of trees and dreams. As it flapped nearer and nearer, the bright colors on it changed like a dark neon rainbow. I reached above me and caught it from the air with my good hand. I gripped it in both hands to read the bright-colored lettering, accidentally smearing blood on it from my busted pinkie.

TONITE (EVERYNITE) ONLY! AT

THE AMPUTEE DISCO ... THE
LORD OF THE GROOVE!

The letters took up most of the paper. In the background were neon silhouettes of people stuck in various dance moves like frozen hip neon shadows. Some walking like Egyptians, some Vogue-ing, some break dancing, some robots, and at least one doing the Soulja Boy. There was more writing, so small I had to squint my bloodshot eyes to read it.

FOLLOW THE CREEK. BEWAREY THE BLADES IN THE CREEK. THE AMPUTEE DISCO ACCEPTS NO RESPONSIBILITY FOR INJURIES RESULTING FROM THE UNDERWATER KNIVES. USE THE BACK DOOR. BEWAREY THE FRONT DOOR. THE AMPUTEE DISCO ACCEPTS NO RESPONSIBILITY FOR INJURIES SUSTAINED FROM USING THE FRONT DOOR. DANCE, MOTHER FUCKER, DANCE.

Suddenly, my urge to hang by my throat was fully outthrobbed by my urge to dance. I walked on the creek bed, careful not to sustain an injury for which no one would be responsible. I cursed my nakedness, because I had nowhere to tuck the flyer. I knew I would want to save it, for its bright colors could light up my dreary room. I'd tack it up between the pages of the medical chart book I'd used as wallpaper. Slowly, I'm learning from the disjointed medicinal pages. The timbulationtis is connected to the feverinactilarious. Instant death occurs in those under

156

eighteen when the two are separated. Cut a man's maitbioica, and he'll bleed out in under a minute. Women over forty are highly likely to bloat and drown in internal bleeding from a good hard kick to the vaculcalra. One day I'll know how to kill us all.

*No one has to die at the dance party*. At least that was what I whispered to myself as I staggered closer to the neon sign.

I heard squawks of different birds and demons seconds before I saw them gathered together, blocking my path. Feathers and scales caught the dying sun and shimmered like drunken memories as the demons and birds danced an awkward circle. As I got closer, I saw the shredded moose corpse around which they danced. The moose carcass had little flesh and much meat, though it steamed and stank, tinted neon green.

*Dear God,* I thought, *they're killing the antlered. Nothing will separate the savages from the heathens now.* My disgust must have read differently on my face, because all three demons gave me high fives as I neared the reeking beast. One was lanky and truck-stop blue. One was chubby and colored bright don't-shootme orange. The last stood my height and was made entirely of TV static. The birds wouldn't stop dancing long enough for me to determine their genusspeciessex, so I quit caring and tried to pass. "What's the rush?" the static demon crackled.

"I'm going to the Amputee Disco," I told him while pointing my thumb at my chest. My mangled pinky flapped obscenely with each self-important prod.

"Aw, gonna groove your troubles away?" the shimmering blue demon asked.

"Well, you know what they say," I answered without slowing my step.

"Of course we know!" the glowing orange demon snarled. He then crossed all four of his knobby arms in a dramatic huff. "We can't get in."

I stopped so quickly that dust formed cocoons over my skidding bare feet.

"No?" I asked over my shoulder.

"We got no moves. We got no game. We are full of squalor and shame," they sang, embracing arm in arm and swaying like sailors on shore leave.

"Why do you think we eat the antlered?" the static demon asked in a buzzing voice of tin.

I turned back away from them. I offered a dismissive shrug so as not to be too rude.

They began clapping and chanting in rhythm.

"We got no moves. We got no game. We are full of squalor and shame."

I wagered a glance back and saw them performing a very well-choreographed team dance. Lots of shucking and jiving. Lots of self-gratification and lying.

"Better hurry, boy! The Lord of the Groove will be on the dance floor soon!" the demon triplets shouted in unison.

"Dance, mother fucker, dance!" squawked the jittery birds.

I heard their song and dance until I took a turn in my ramshackle path and was face to snout with a black dog. He stood on his hind feet and leaned with one paw on the trunk of a mighty cedar. His eyes were mismatched: one gunmetal blue and the other a bright rainbow of neons. Staring at him, shaggy and dark, made me think of sweet January—her tattered past and patchwork present.

"The fuck?" he asked with a snout nod.

I didn't know how to answer him and decided I would cave his skull in with a rock before I would retort. I'd be clever after the fact and spit my response at his mangled carcass. I looked all around me for a rock with enough heft to do the trick. I saw a few and picked them up. I did little test clubs in the air, but none held up to my low standards. It was high school all over again. Rocks and obsessions will always let you down. Without a suitable weapon, I had no choice but to engage the canine in conversation.

"The fuck you asking?" I answered with a chin nod.

"You don't have to be so rude." He pushed away from the tree and spun around to drop onto all fours. "I'm not the one you try to strangle away from your thoughts."

He saw me in one eye and my sins with the other. That eye teared up.

I thought of sexy January, so burnt raw and enthralling.

"I'm not going to apologize unless I have to. It's a game I play with things that I want to kill," I said as I inched past him, careful not to let my manhood dangle too close to his tooth-lined mouth.

"You can't go into the Amputee Disco all dick-swinging," he informed me with a wink.

I again cursed my nakedness. I—also again—looked for a rock capable of shattering dog skull to shards. This time, I found one. I whistled softly to taunt my innocence as I knelt and wrapped my finger around it. My broken pinkie smeared blood across the dry surface of my chosen tool. I tested its weight. I approved its sharp edges and feel in my palm. I stood, still whistling, and noticed that the black dog no longer stood behind me.

Instead, a man in an orange-and-purple jogging suit stood in his place. His eyes screamed his confusion, and his mouth stuttered to form words. I knew how it felt to be lost in the forest. Unwilling to waste my perfect skull-splitting rock, I cracked him as hard as I could in his forehead. His eyes rolled up as if watching his skull cave in from the inside. His knees buckled in perfect synchronization. I caught his collar and gave him a few more skull fractures before dropping him to the creek-side.

"I would have done it if I had hands." The black dog had returned and stood looking at his traitorous paws.

"The honest ones make me nervous," I brazenly explained.

He shrugged and spoke again. "At least now we both get what we need. You got some hip new clothes to wear at the Amputee Disco, and I get new human skin."

I tugged off the dead man's pants without a word. They fit better than I had hoped. I unzipped his jacket and had to flop him over to get both his arms out. I put it on and found it fit perfectly as well. I zipped it all the way up, then unzipped it halfway down my chest. I looked at the black dog as he stood staring and salivating at the naked corpse.

"Aren't you gonna get your new skin?" I asked him while adjusting my crotch in the silky purple pants.

"That's kinda personal, don't you think? Besides, you better get to the Amputee Disco before the Lord of the Groove goes on." He wiped away pink drool with his front paw and turned his mismatched eyes back to me.

"Dance, mother fucker, dance," he offered me as I walked down the path to the Amputee Disco.

I tracked close to the water, losing myself in its cold, wet culling song. Dreams and memories rolled together, penetrating and infecting one another until my every thought was a bastardized mutant existing only to claw at my feeble sanity. My lips went numb, and I tasted rosy toxic chlorine. I thought of sweet January, the blood dripping from her lips and the sting of her backhand.

A few more twists and turns of staggering over rottedsoft logs, and I came to the clearing aglow with the lights flashing on the Amputee Disco. Aside from the fact that it was draped in hundreds of strings of neon lights, it was just a large, square metal-panel-covered barn.

A long line of the trendiest people I've ever seen stood side by side in a looping queue that disappeared into the tall pines of the forest. They all drank glowing drinks that a buzzard served them from a wobbly tray he balanced on his head and beak. The blaring neons of the signs stole the light from the shadows. It gave me the feeling of being locked in a neon cage. I just went with it.

The doors were missing, and instead, two giant metallic tubes covered in fierce flesh-rending spikes spun so quickly that they hummed an eerie hateful dirge. The first two people in line, a fellow in a bright white suit with a glow-in-the-dark green tie and a woman in a low-hanging fringe-lined neon paisley blouse and a pair of Daisy Dukes, stepped forward, waving their arms as they chatted aloud about meaningless bullshit.

They raised and lowered their feet in perfect synchronization right into the spinning grinder-doorway. The couple slammed together as the wheels shredded them into one shimmering, fashionable pulp. Flecks of stubborn flesh and neon ichor speckled the next two people in line—a man with tall neonblue hair and leather pants, and a woman in torn jeans covered in glowing patches and a leather tube top. They ignored the gore

162

shower and stepped forward. They repeated the process, the only difference between the two couples being the meaningless bullshit about which they were chattering as they fed themselves to the deadly doorway.

I looked over the line of people all dressed so trendybright and noticed for the first time the two demons standing on either side of the line as it emerged from the tree line. A small demon with long skinny legs stood on a barstool. He held a sign that read "Be A Responsible Bleeder" scrawled in black Sharpie marker. The other demon was squat and scaly, and he tortured a much smaller barstool. As the couples in line approached him, he held out a three-fingered hand and collected a small handful of cash. He tucked the money into his neon yellow vest. SECURITY was emblazoned across the back in bright orange lettering.

I walked up to him, feeling underdressed in my neon running suit. I kicked the drink-serving vulture and giggled as he flapped his wings to steady the tray. He squawked obscenities at me while I tapped the security demon on his knobby shoulder.

His barstool squealed like metal on metal as he grunted and rolled around to face me. He burped a greeting at me that may have been, "What?"

"Is this the front door?" I asked while jerking a thumb at the trendy-people-eater behind me.

"Yup," the security demon belched again.

"Don't these people know about the back door?" I whispered conspiratorially into his malformed ear.

He shrugged his hunched and bumpy shoulders. He tilted his head back and forth a few times like he was trying to shake the right words out. No words tumbled free, and he pointed to the demon with the sign. He was now clutching a sign that said, "Some People Don't Know the Difference Between a Meat Grinder and a Good Time" in black marker.

A wave of understanding punished me. The hip, the cool, the super-neat were all feeding themselves to the giant grinder at an alarming speed. As I watched twosome after twosome slam into each other as the wheels chewed them up, I heard the muffled bass reverberating from the metal-paneled shack. My toes tapped involuntarily. I felt the groove in my shattered pinkie, and it danced through me. My arms floated in the air and then swooped back down as I did a one-man wave.

"Nice moves," the security demon grumbled. "Back door is right around that far corner. You'll see all the regulars. Clyde the Stump and the Abortion Twins and all the rest should be back there." He stared at me for a minute, and I saw his bulging purple eyes count each of my digits and limbs. "But I can tell you ain't no regular. First-timer, huh? Fresh meat!"

He leaned forward to slap his knee, tears twinning his laughter as two women walked arm in arm into the grinder. When they slammed together, one slipped on the gore-slick ground, throwing her friend face-first into the grinder and herself sprawling backwards. Her scream drilled the air, and the volume of the bass inside increased with it. The woman dropped her glowing drink, and the liquid sizzled and bubbled on the forest floor. She reached toward the two people behind her, two men in matching neon-orange and neon-blue tuxedos, panic bursting the blood vessels in her eyes.

There was a murmur through the line. Discontent at the disco. The demon, still chuckling under his garbage breath, shimmied off his stool and waddled to the front of the line. I followed him.

He tapped the gentlemen in the neon-blue tuxedo on the shoulder. The man turned, took notice of the demon, and removed his top hat in an extravagant bow. The demon returned the bow in a manner both vulgar and grandiose before stepping past the man. He shrugged his shoulders at the man while placing his large warty foot on the screaming girl's forehead.

"Wait! Don't!" She abandoned her escape from the spinning gears and focused on getting his foul foot off her face. "Help me! We just want to dance!"

"Well," the demon chortled as he used his foot to shove her far enough into the gears for them to catch the meat of her leg. "Show 'em what you're made of!"

She screamed as the gears sucked her in, peeling flesh from bone as she disappeared. Her screams morphed to highpitched garbles. The tuxedoed men covered their

165

ears with gloved hands until the grinder finished pulping her. The bouncer demon shrugged again and motioned me in front of the waiting men. I don't bow to strangers, but I offered a nod as I cut past them. They scoffed in return.

"Using the back door," the man in the orange tux told the other, "what a godless heathen."

"Indeed," the man in the blue tux answered. "His mother would shit on her master's face if she knew!"

They continued the scatological mother insults as they walked smugly into the door gears. Pulpy ribbons of flesh and neon-orange and -blue tuxedos spat at me as I rounded the corner, ready to get down to some serious dancing.

There was no line at the back door. No meat grinder either. The smaller demon from the front of the bar stood perched on a barstool. He held a sign that read, "Dance, Mother Fucker, Dance." Light prismed on the ground and trees from the open doorway as if a million disco balls rotated in the room beyond. Rhythm and sin crawled out in waves, caressing me in their beat. I nodded at the sign-toting demon, and he nodded back. I winked, and he winked. I smiled, and he leaped off his stool and disappeared around the corner without a word.

I walked through the simple door into a room a dozen times the size of the building that housed it. I took a step, and a mountain of a man stepped from the shadows to my left. He held up the club of a fingerless stump. With his other hand—only missing two fingers—he handed me another flyer, a straight razor, and a drink voucher. I held all three in my hands and stared dumbly at them. The music pounded my thoughts to senseless mush, and the lights stole my concentration like Ritalin withdrawals.

"First time?" the bouncer asked in a voice as deep as the thudding bass of the disco.

I swallowed the lump of trepidation clawing its way up my dry throat and nodded.

"Well, you'll dig it. I see it in your eyes. You'll be a regular soon." His face split in a smile, and I noticed his lack of lips.

"A regular?" I asked nervously. "Like Clyde the Stump?"

"Oh, yeah! Just like Clyde the Stump!" His laugh was wheezy and dead, but honest. "You picked a good night, a lot of people here to dance tonight. The Lord of the Groove will be pleased."

I held up the razor so the reflection of the lights could dance on the deathly sharp blade. "Do I need this?"

"Yup, you'll know when the time comes," he tells me with a sheen of malice on his eyeballs. "Now get in there and groove, man!"

He grabbed me by the scruff of my neck and threw me into the glowing room. I landed on my face before crawling to the nearest wall. I sat against the wall and noticed the large tubes running all over the ceiling and walls. Some were as small as a lady's wrist and others as wide as small automobiles. Glowing chunks of gore pushed through the tubes, soaking the massive room in grotesque light. My eyes wandered to the dance floor, where I observed dozens of dark dancing shapes. None danced the same way or even to the same beat. Each person lost to his own groove, awash in pulsing rhythm and glowing innards. Each of them was missing at least one limb, no shadowy figure complete.

I wanted nothing more than to dance with them.

I folded the flyer in half and tucked it into my pocket. My wall would retain the memory for me alongside my tedious medical-chart wallpaper. I stood up with the straight razor in one hand and the drink coupon in the other. The groove sensed my trepidation to join the pounding aural bacchanal, and it tugged me forward onto the massive dance floor. A woman en route to the bar crashed into me and knocked me into her destination.

Pain flared up my back and down my spine as our momentum drove a cluster of my tragnibulous nerves hard into the stainless-steel bar. The music increased in volume and pressure. The glow, incredibly bright as it was, became pleasantly blinding. A silky tingle followed the pain, engulfing my body into murky numbness. My eyes rolled back in ecstasy. My head flopped forward, a sandbag held on a weed.

My blurring eyes took in the sight of the feminine battering ram. She had long black hair pulled tight on the top of her head. Several streaks of different neon colors glowed in the light of the iridescent guts. I noticed she was missing one ear. Her face was smooth and slender, a vision of cruel beauty, scarred with dozens of bulging x-shaped scars. She wore a tight neon bikini that highlighted the fact that she only had one sadly perfect breast. Her stomach and half her ribcage were missing. Two shimmering metal rods took their place, fused to her porcelain flesh and keeping her one wonderful breast held high. As my senses stabilized from the euphoria that chased my pain, I realized I was grinding my semi-hard cock onto her hip.

She winked one silver-blue eye at me and shifted her hip away from me. She immediately replaced it with her knee. The hard bone of her kneecap crushed my delicates as one fleshy bouquet. The pain twisted my stomach and curled my toes. She shoved my hunched form into the bar as the silky numbness radiated from my crushed genitals throughout my entire body.

Wracked with the dual sensations of stomach-turning pain and near-ejaculatory pleasure, I gasped to the bartender, "Who is that?"

"Mmmphm Obfooo Fitaaa, Jciooo," was his distorted and muffled reply.

I blinked away my obvious tears and turned to look at him. He was nearly as large as the man at the front door. The reason for his garbled talk was evident, as he had no lower jaw. He smiled a toothy grin at me with his upper lip. He stood wiping a mug clean with hands each a few fingers short.

"Did that hurt?" I asked, pointing at my chin and then

his lack of chin.

"Dfph hmmph hmmmph?" he asked back, nodding at my crotch.

"He asked if that hurt," a small yellow chickadee spoke from his shoulder. "You know, when Jacinda knocked you in the rocks?"

"At first," I told the jawless bartender and translating chickadee. Then, "Her name is Jacinda?"

"Yup. She is one of the Abortion Twins. There's her sister, Amy." The bird spoke, but the man pointed to a big girl flailing in rotund glory on the dance floor. Where slender Jacinda had only two rods implanted in place of lower ribs, hefty Amy had over a dozen sturdy shimmering rods holding up her lone bulging breast. Her hair was as wild and unruly as Jacinda's was smooth and tightly done. I shivered at the sight of her jiggling to the overpowering groove.

I put the straight razor in my pocket. I slid the drink voucher across the cold surface of the bar to the bar man. "Scotch and gasoline, please."

"Fuffh," the jawless man said.

"Sure," the chickadee translated.

The man handed me a tall glass filled with ice cubes, Johnnie Walker Red, and high-grade unleaded. I stirred it with my flopping pinkie and bobbed my head to the surrounding musical sounds. Chunks of jagged torn flesh and slivers of bone spun like a toxic tornado inside my glass. The sting of gas on open wound turned to silky tickles as it danced slowly up my arm

"Stay away from Jacinda," a whiny voice spoke from next to me. I turned on my stool to face the voice, but no one was there. The voice spoke again. "I said stay away from Jacinda."

The second time, I realized the voice was coming from a limbless man wrapped in neon sheets and lying on a small couch facing the dance floor. He bore a strong resemblance to the Americanized Jesus, with his long sandy hair framing his bearded pale face. His faith lost like his limbs. I knew without introduction that I was in the presence of Clyde the Stump.

I opened my mouth to tell him about January—her sweet, burning, and hateful love—but he stuck out his tongue and spat at me.

"I don't want ta' hear your bullshit excuses. Just stay the fuck away from Jacinda." His eyes shone in the hot glow, his feelings leaking down his cheeks. Salty insecurities soaked his beard and glimmered in the glow.

"Okay." I nodded. Uncomfortable in his furious glare, I then told him, "Well, I better get out on the dance floor."

The groove wrapped me in its pulsing embrace, and I floated onto the dance floor, away from the angry stump of a man.

My arms flew wildly. My hands clenched and unclenched. Blood trickled from my destroyed pinkie finger and flung like a blood sprinkler. My feet kicked and slid. My knees popped and locked. I bobbed my head; I banged my head. My eyes crossed, rolled, closed. The light shone through my closed eyelids and soaked into my soul. I felt the heat of life and the tremble of future in each pulse of the groove. The music possessed innumerable hands, and they pinched me, tickled me, and stroked me. My muscles burned from the exertion, each sharp burning ache followed by numbness and tingling.

Every jerk was torture unbearable; every shimmy was pleasure incarnate.

And I danced.

Danced.

Danced.

I danced right into Jacinda and Amy. They wrapped around me like tentacled nightmares, crushing and humping to the twisted beats and bombast. My groove couldn't be thwarted, despite their assassination attempts, but I couldn't shake them off either. I smelled peppermint and death on their breaths. Brimstone and piss reeked from their hair. Calamity and lust were their sweat, which they smeared all over me. I breathed it in and thought of January, her jealous silence and laser-beam eyes.

The music reached a sudden extravagant and excessive climax.

I was swimming in the tinny silence that erupted in the music's wake when Clyde the Stump screamed, "Stay the fuck away from Jacinda!"

172

As suddenly as it had ceased, the music began again. It was utter aural chaos. Every instrument I had ever known, and several I had never dared to imagine, each blasted out its own slightly different tune. The crowded dance floor raised their stumps in the air and screamed as one, both terrifying and terrified.

A colossal beast stood in the middle of the crowd. The Lord of the Groove had taken the floor. It was a massive, hideous golem of volunteered human flesh, composed of the limbs sacrificed to it. A hundred legs kicked under a hundred arms to the wail of the tempest of sound. Three heads sat lumpish on top of the hundred arms, each head made from smaller pieces—ears, hands, feet, dicks, and breasts.

Jacinda and Amy tore off their clothes and then tore at mine as the Lord of the Groove danced in monstrous malevolence before us. The music wrapped around us, but we sank into shadows as the glow of the massive room crowded to bathe the Lord of the Groove in its grotesque glare.

The Lord of the Groove danced for us. We danced for the Lord of the Groove.

Its dead arms waved, and amputees on the floor waved back. Its feet shuffled and hopped; the half that could not reach the floor flailed endlessly. The clubgoers shuffled and hopped in response. Chaos beats, chaos god, chaos fashion. As my eyes rolled, I caught sight of rainbow reflections cast from razor blades as they slapped open throughout the club.

The Lord of the Groove danced for us. We danced for the Lord of the Groove.

The giant-flesh-dance-god shook and jerked, and everybody cut. Jacinda carved a heart on her lone breast. Amy attacked her own swollen, fat breast with reckless abandon, slicing it in a half-dozen places. A man with only one hand rocked back and forth on the ground, shouting "whoot, whoot!" as he worked at his ankle like a lumberjack with an ax on a white pine. A man with no arms below his elbows writhed in panic Tantric motions while a woman took two razor blades to his genitals with warm maniacal glee. I looked to the bar at the exact moment the jawless bartender reached up and sliced off an ear.

Everyone threw their severed limbs at the Lord of the Groove. They flicked the blood off their hands and stumps in the direction of the grooving abomination. The dance-god caught the flung flesh offerings and swallowed them down one of the mouths in his malformed heads. I watched as body parts regurgitated and sprouted from the flesh god, kicking and waving as if still connected to their previous owners.

Moans joined the chaotic beats as everybody carved flesh. The music warped with the moans, making the entire experience dirge-like and bloody.

As everyone around me removed limbs and inflicted grievous acts of self-mutilation for the Lord of the

Groove, I thought of January, her bright purple scars and cold dead heart. All at once, the dance seemed so foolish.

Jacinda's eyes caressed me and noticed I had no fresh wound to offer their hideous heathen god. She rubbed the flat side of her razor against herself, from the inside of her thigh, up her pussy lips, up and around the glowing rod supporting her breast, then around her bright pink nipple before slashing it toward my face. I reached my hand up and caught the blade a scant millimeter from my cheek. We winked at each other, and I broke her wrist. She howled in pain, then moaned in ecstasy.

The cries of Clyde the Stump cut through the throbbing music. "I told you to stay away from Jacinda! What the fuck is wrong with you?"

I turned from Jacinda as she swayed to the errant beat, clutching her flopping wrist. I was surrounded by people dripping sweat and blood. It occurred to me as they killed me with their eyes that I had to pay the cover charge. Jacinda spun me around by my shoulder and pointed at my mangled pinky.

"Give the Lord of the Groove your pinky finger! It hangs broken, begging for offering!"

Blood from the heart on her breast dripped down, giving her nipple a crimson sheen. The shadow of the Lord of the Groove engulfed her. The god stood behind her, still convulsing to the ragtag grooves as she glared at me.

*A little flesh sacrifice never hurt anyone,* I reasoned with myself. Then I lopped off my pinky finger with my straight razor. The crowd cheered. The Lord of the Groove showed its vapid approval by shaking its multitude of arms and legs in my direction.

I held my severed pinky in my fist and thought of January, her murderous love and steadfast soul feasting.

The crowd pressed against me in anticipation of me throwing my sacrifice to the Lord of the Groove. Instead, I tucked it into my pocket. I turned to leave the dance floor and the Amputee Disco. The crowd grumbled their disapproval and reached for me with hands missing fingers and fresh bleeding stumps. I clutched tight my razor and slashed them back away, each wracked with pain and pleasure. I walked, razor swiping, through their ranks 'til I reached the bar. The bartender frowned at me, and the chickadee shit down the bartender's chest.

"You can't leave without paying the cover," the chickadee told me.

I saw the seriousness in the jawless bar man's quivering eyes. I heard sobbing from next to me and noticed Clyde the Stump, shaken free of his glowing robes, with tears and snot coating his face. The Lord of the Groove danced through the crowd after me. It trampled dancers too slow to avoid it under its hundred stomping feet. Its hundred flailing arms tossed amputees left and right as it cleared a swath of destruction behind me.

One of its hideous patchwork heads leaned toward me as if to gobble me up for my blasphemy. In one smooth motion, I reached down, grabbed Clyde by his shoulder

176

stumps, and swung him leg-stumps-first into the Lord of the Groove's gaping gullet. The severed-limb golem quivered and jerked as Clyde wiggled and squirmed to escape his demise. The paraplegic slipped just far enough to gag his god. The monster's hundred arms all reached for Clyde's flopping form, but none of them could grip the hysterical man-gag. The Lord of the Groove's other two heads deflated in on themselves, and the head with the Clyde-gag grew larger. Instead of being expelled, Clyde slipped down just a little bit more, completely blocking the terrible deity's airway.

The dance-god swayed, jerked impossibly, and tipped over backwards, crushing the crazed followers behind it under a mountain of their own severed limbs. All at once, the perverted orchestra of sound ground to an ear-slipping halt.

The silence was as deafening and chaotic as the music was seconds before. Then the buzzing silence was shattered as dancers began screaming their loss and agony. They converged on their fallen god and beat Clyde with their fists and stumps, trying to force him down into dance-god belly. Clyde was far too stuck, and he screamed hoarsely for Jacinda as the crowd beat his face and head to blubbering pulp. The hundred arms and hundred legs of the Lord of the Groove were slowing, freezing one by one. I smelled panic in the sweat haze of the dance floor. Soon they were plucking out the Lord of the Groove's finger-eyeballs and filling the several empty sockets with freshly severed limbs in hopes of reviving the monstrosity.

Jacinda wept and shrieked as she carved strips of her scalp to throw at the twitching dance-god. Amy reached over and cut Jacinda's hand off at her shattered wrist. The hand dropped to the blood-slick floor, still clutching the length of neon-orange hair and scalp skin it was going to offer. Jacinda screamed and didn't stop screaming. No wave of euphoria followed the pain, and she slashed her heavyset sister across her throat. A torrent of blood gushed down Amy's ample bosom and sprayed the unmoving arms of the fallen god. With her last choking breath, Amy flung her razor to her side and gave her twin a matching mortal wound. Both of the Abortion Twins fell into the dead arms of their god as they bled out on the dance floor. The remaining amputees were behaving in the same way, and the bloodshed was as all encompassing as the eerie glow from all around. The bouncer from the front door climbed up the god corpse and began chewing on the stiff fingers, swallowing each, bone and all. Amidst the carnage, I reached down and picked up Jacinda's severed hand. I uncurled her three-fingered fist, and I stole the brightly colored lock of hair. I used my razor to trim the unsightly head flesh away, then tied a length of hair in a bow around my severed pinkie.

I gave it to January as a gift with the promise that I'd never dance again.

# SOUL IN MY THROAT

I should have put her soul in a glass jar. It would have stained the jar black, just like all the others. I know that now. She smelled so pure and so sweet.

Sometimes gristle looks just like meat.

I tasted her—her sweat and her blood. My stomach turned, and I couldn't resist. I took out her eyes, and they tasted fine. But her soul was poisoned and foul.

My eyes water, and I'm dying now.

I cut off her hands and hung them with the others. The black jars swirled and shone there on my shelf. Thick blood caked in stripes down her cheeks, and I didn't notice her grin.

I save the souls, and I eat the sin.

Her soul was swollen, as decay made it bloat. It chokes down my screams and my breath. My hands and feet go numb first. My knife clatters when it hits the floor, and the jars seem to rattle. My world is going as black as the jars upon my shelf. Her eyeless corpse smiles at me while I choke on her soul in my throat.

# SO PROUDLY THEY CRAWL

## SAFE HOUSE

Ben's pulse races, and his heartbeat throbs in his ears. His knuckles are clenched so tight on the steering wheel that his fingertips are numb. Adrenaline tints his vision red, and he takes deep breaths every few seconds to try to calm himself down. The thick black wool stocking cap he wears is damp with nervous sweat from his bald head. He drives the stolen moving truck off the highway onto a dirt road and then, after a bumpy twentyminute jaunt, into the small abandoned town of Jason's Prayer.

Ben knows it is just his nerves, but he still hears police sirens behind them as they stroll down the barren Main Street. His eyes dart back and forth at the decrepit buildings facing the street. All look long abandoned, but only a few have boards nailed up across the windows. Those windows left unboarded somehow also remain unbroken, a fact that amazes Ben. He is used to seeing graffiti and other, more creative, forms of vandalism everywhere he goes in the city. Not that the buildings look welcoming; each is visibly crumbling and stained a mysterious black in places. The blacktop road has been neglected for so long that it has disintegrated, for the most part, and given way to weeds and bramble bushes. As the truck dodges larger bushes, the entire town gives the impression that a loud noise could cause it all to crumble down around them.

"Relax," Jimmy says from the seat next to him. "No one has even thought about this town for decades. Ain't no way the cops are gonna find us."

"What happened here?" Ben notices the slight whine of fear tinting his voice, so he quickly clears his throat and tries again. "Where did everybody go?"

"Don't know, don't care," Jimmy answers dismissively.

"Well how the hell did you find it?"

Jimmy shifts his eyes to Ben and lets menace resonate in his glare. "Uncle Rex used to bring his 'problems' here."

Ben decides quickly that he doesn't want to push the subject any further. It's bad enough he's ended up owing Jimmy Haas, a.k.a. Jimmy Scissors, so much money that he is being forced to serve as the wheel man for his homicidal band of thieves to pay it all off. The last thing he wants is anything to do with Jimmy's infamous Uncle Rex, a.k.a. Sexy Rexy. Rex also happens to be the leader of Hitler's Hammer: a racist cult of demented rednecks and skinheads that controls a small army of meth-head Satanists throughout the area.

"Left here," Jimmy nods, "and then take the second right. Follow that until you come to the big crumbling bastard surrounded by trees."

Jimmy's description of the safe building was fairly apt, though painted with clumsy, dumb words. The building is set back within a ring of three-hundred-foot-tall trees and seems to be in worse condition than any other building in the decaying town. It is three stories tall, but most of the roof has collapsed down into the rooms on the third floor. Huge cracks rise up the outer walls from the foundation, and each crack is rimmed with the same strange black stain as the buildings in town. Every window is broken. The sun shines through the trees that surround the massive building, casting shadows that stalk through the hidden rooms. Ben looks for the name on the building and notices that the wall around the front entrance has crumbled in and is blocked with a blackened pile of rubble.

"What did this use to be?" Ben asks as he slows down, looking for a place to park.

"This piece of shit used to be a building." Jimmy laughs like a knife in the ears at his joke and continues, "Don't park here. Follow that half-assed path all the way around back."

Ben does as he is told and drives the length of the building. He follows a barely visible path through the tall weeds. Out of the corners of his eyes, he sees movement inside the building, and he slams on the brakes when he thinks he sees a malformed face gazing back at him—for only a split second—from a first-floor window.

"What the fuck, Ben?" Jimmy Scissors glares at Ben and looks ready to stick a penknife between his ribs.

"I saw something," Ben says. "In there."

The scowl doesn't leave Jimmy's face, but he turns slowly to look in the window Ben indicates. He keeps distrustful eyes on Ben until his head is almost all the way turned. He leans forward, flexing his steroid-infused muscles, and blocks Ben's view with the solid black swastika tattooed on the back of his bald head. At first, the skinhead sees nothing. Then the shadows from the trees move, and he thinks he catches a glimpse of something. Something white and quick flashes in the back of the room- Clang! Clang! Clang!

The four men in the back of the moving truck pound on the steel wall separating them. Jimmy and Ben both jump at the thunderous sound. Ben turns red and lets his foot off the brake. Jimmy feels embarrassed, and it turns instantly to anger. He pounds back twice as hard.

"Shut the fuck up, ya mooks!" he screams at the metal wall loudly enough to make Ben wince. The "mooks" in the back simmer down, and Ben pulls the moving van around the corner.

The back lot is crowded with cars. Some crushed and stacked and some that would be in perfect condition, had it not been for forty-plus years of the elements, parked in neat little rows. The path becomes more defined and leads into the maze of ancient vehicles. The path pulls them farther from the building as stacks of crushed cars line most of the back wall. Ben drives slowly, dodging bumpers that have rusted enough to fall and block the road. Once clear of the maze, Ben sees the built-on parking structure in which he is supposed to park. He pulls the truck up to a faded wooden door, and Jimmy pounds on the wall.

"Open the door, Riggs!"

Ben and Jimmy sit and wait while Riggs jumps out of the back of the truck and jogs up to the door. He has already changed out of his job gear—with the exception of the black combat boots they always wear—and is back in blue jeans, red suspenders, and white t-shirt. Riggs's head has more stubble than Jimmy's, but he is just as muscled and aggressive as his lifelong pal. He pulls a key ring from his back pocket and unfastens a small lock on the door. He tucks the lock in his pocket and swings the door open. Ben drives into the crumbling garage, and Riggs pulls the door closed behind them. Ben kills the ignition, and the other three men jump out of the back of the truck.

Casper and Seth both stretch their muscled tattoo-covered arms as they walk around to the front of the van to meet Jimmy and Riggs. Dennis thunders out of the back of the truck with a bottle of Jim Beam and his suspenders hanging down around his hips. Dennis is the only one with facial hair, and his graying handlebar mustache is wet with the whiskey as he joins the others.

"Damn good job, brothers," Dennis slurs. "To Dewayne!" He guzzles the Jim Beam, spilling it down his neck and chest as he swallows.

The other men—besides Jimmy—all regard him coldly but echo, "To Dewayne," and each takes a pull off the bottle. Dewayne was the last member of their crew, and he caught a bullet in the face during the armored-car holdup. He got the driver's-side door open, but the driver answered back with automatic rifle fire, splattering Dewayne's brains and bits of his skull out of the back of his face shield. Jimmy was right behind him and sank three rapid-fire gut shots into the driver before pulling him out to the concrete and popping one more into his forehead. Dennis stomped the bullet-torn corpse until Casper and Riggs dragged him to the back of the armored truck. Minutes later, they were switching cargo into the moving van and setting off an explosion that leveled an abandoned hotel.

"Yeah, good job," Jimmy says, neither his eyes nor his tone impressed with Dennis's reaction to Dewayne's death. "Now let's unload this shit."

Jimmy leads the men to the rear of the truck, and he starts pointing and giving orders.

"I want our supplies taken to the biggest room on the second floor; you can't miss it." He nods to Ben, who nods back but waits 'til all the orders are given before moving.

"I want these sacks of cash taken to the shitter on the first floor. We'll divvy up as soon as we get settled in." He nods to Seth, Casper, and a drunk and distracted Dennis.

"Me and Riggs will move this last case." Ben looks past him and sees the large metal crate he is talking about. It takes up much more room than the bags of cash and has both German and American decals emblazoned across its smooth metal surface. Jimmy catches him looking, and he leans down, blocking Ben's view. The corners of Jimmy's mouth twitch menacingly, and Ben grabs three packs and turns away.

"All right?" Jimmy asks.

"Right!" all the other men answer.

Ben wrestles the three hockey bags up a creaking flight of stairs and finds "the big room" right away. Sunlight shines through the windows, giving the green walls of the large room a soft, squishy look. Bumps and tears in the wall give the impression of something trying to escape from them. Most of the floor is covered with an inch of standing water that reeks of rodent piss and decay. Ceiling tiles hang down from above, revealing only darkness. Several others litter the floor, halfdissolved in the water. Directly across from him, Ben sees a door built into the far wall. Two matching cabinets are set on either side of the door, both with their doors slightly open. Ben wades through the muck and drops all three hockey bags on one of the cabinets before turning back for the other bags.

Ben works his way through the devastated building, back to the garage. The floors creak and pop as he moves. Shadows slink in doorways to darkened rooms, and Ben can hear footfalls and grunting as the others work. He gets back down to the garage to find everyone else gone. He walks to the back of the truck, sees it's still half full of money bags, and decides to check out the garage before he takes his last load up. A great big cloth tarp halves the garage, and Ben chooses to start his exploring there. He pushes the tarp to one side and walks through.

## DENNIS

Casper and Seth each grab as many bags of cash as they can carry. Dennis takes two bags and his bottle of Jim Beam. Most of the first floor is flooded, and a thick black stain covers the majority of the walls. The three men walk without talking, the noise of their feet stalking through the mess the only sound. They hear footfalls above them and exchange nervous glances.

Realizing Jimmy is out of earshot, Casper speaks first.

"Where the fuck are we?"

"The ground floor, dumbass." Seth chuckles.

Casper shoots him a glare, and Seth's smile fades. "I don't know, Casper."

"How the fuck long are we gonna be in this trash heap?"

"Well, as fucked as shit got back in town …" Seth starts, but Dennis interrupts.

"You mean as fucked as Dewayne got back in town, don't ya?"

"That's not what I'm saying, Dennis."

"The fuck it ain't!"

Dennis's anger flushes his face, and he slams his two bags of cash into Casper's chest. The other two skinheads laugh at him, and he flips them the bird as he turns back the way they came.

"Where the hell do you think you're going?" Seth calls after him.

"To think about Dewayne and get drunk. You got a fucking problem with that?"

"Shit," Casper answers, "We don't, but we ain't speaking for Jimmy Scissors."

Without turning around, Dennis grumbles, "Fuck Jimmy Scissors. He got my best friend killed."

"Your fucking funeral!" Seth hollers at his back as the haggard man disappears into the shadows.

"Keep pushing, dickhead, and we'll only have to split it five ways!" Casper punctuates his shout with braying laughter.

Dennis ignores the taunts and sloshes through the darkness, gripping his bottle of whiskey like it is his only friend in the world. He takes a few awkward steps, then takes a chug off the bottle, repeating the process across the rotting first floor. He sobs and curses in the darkness, oblivious to the shifting shapes occupying the shadows around him, lost in his misery. Dennis leans against the wall and uses it to navigate the dark hallway in which he has found himself. He reaches a door and pauses long enough to light a cigar he pulls from the pocket of his camo pants. He pulls deep on the cigar, takes a massive swallow of whiskey, and then exhales thick smoke into whatever room he leans against. He pushes the door in and flinches from the bright afternoon sun that greets him through the shattered window inside. The floor of the room is covered with slimy black feces, and the wall is covered in crude fecal art of SS and swastika symbols. Dennis feels the whiskey warming his belly begin a slow, slick crawl up his throat, and he takes a deep pull off the cigar to stifle it. He blows a puff of smoke into the room and watches it drift upwards to a hole in the ceiling. A shiver wracks Dennis, and he slams the door as he storms past it.

Dennis loved Dewayne, and Dewayne loved Dennis. Dewayne was the only person Dennis ever loved. Dennis had grown up in a white-power camp and had been taught to reject anyone who wasn't like him. His antisocial attitude eventually landed him in prison for beating a young Mexican kid half to death with a two-by-four at a sheetrock jobsite. He ended up sharing a cell with

Dewayne, and over the next ten years, their friendship grew into an awkward romance. Due to the aggressive ignorance of their youth, their relationship was always rocky and violent but, for the most part, a total secret. Once they counted down their days and hit the streets again, no one questioned their decision to be roommates. No one ever suspected their secret, but just lately, Jimmy had been looking at them differently. Curious glances that bounced back and forth and made Dennis uncomfortable.

"Fucking Jimmy," he slurs as he stumbles forward, "killing fucking Dewayne. That shit ain't right. Fucking bullshit. I'll kill you, Jimmy Fucking Haas." He gags again, half from the whiskey and half from the lingering reek of shit.

Jimmy changed the plan at the last minute. Dewayne was supposed to go to the other door and kill the guard riding shotgun, but Jimmy tapped him on the shoulder and pointed him to his death instead. Dewayne ran up to the door and cast a pale face to Dennis before he yanked it open. Dennis saw fear under the glare of his face shield. Dennis takes a chug to wash the memory away. He kicks a chunk of ceiling tile, and it sails into the darkness right ahead of him. He hears it hit the wall with a wet thwack and then peel and fall off the wall. He doesn't hear it land.

He kicks a rusted can, and it disappears into the darkness, but only a series of faint growls sounds in its absence. Dennis gnaws on the butt of his cigar and pulls the gun from his waistband. He takes slow, staggered steps forward, squishing obscenely, the only light from the glowing tip of his cigar. His eyes adjust enough for him to see an open door in front of him. He notices a small desk, broken in half, in the hallway next to him, and he reaches over to rifle through an open drawer for a scrap of paper. He tucks his gun next to his prick and picks the bottle of whiskey back up. The scrap of paper catches flame quickly when Dennis holds it up to the cherry end of his smoke. He smiles around the cigar and holds the poor-man's torch up in front of him.

Dennis notices first that the open doorway is actually an open elevator shaft. Before he can see the dozens of hideous creatures, legless and pale, clutched to the inside of the shaft by their muscular arms, a thick hand grabs him by his throat. Razorlike claws dig into his neck, and blood trickles down the hand and drips down the elevator shaft. His arm swings up out of instinct, and the flame casts a light on the monster gripping his throat. Three eyes glare back at him, one from the middle of the humanoid forehead, each hate-filled and alien. Two small holes under the eyes flare as the creature inhales the rich scent of Dennis's claret draining from his veins. The monster opens his mouth, and Dennis sees rows of buzz-saw teeth. He gags on cigar smoke and blood. The hand around his throat yanks him forward into the elevator shaft. He drops the torch, but a creature reaches up with twitchy sped and slams it out before it falls more than two feet past Dennis's dangling, kicking feet. He bites the tip off the cigar when he feels the monsters grab onto him. He feels their weight as they pull and rip at him in their primal greed. The hand around his throat yanks again, this time upward, and his head is torn away with it. The monsters hanging in the shaft devour the rest of the corpse before it can continue its descent. The empty whiskey bottle falls past the feasting beasts and shatters on the basement floor far below.

## HAAS FAMILY HISTORY

Jimmy and Riggs wait for everyone else to grab their first loads before they work the metal case out of the truck. It isn't nearly as heavy as it looks, but Jimmy sits on it and lights a smoke as soon as they drop it out.

"Break time already?" Riggs snorts.

"I'm in no rush," Jimmy says while exhaling a cloud of smoke. "Besides, I don't wanta wake Grandpa."

Riggs wrinkles his face and lets his expression ask the question for him. Jimmy is used to the look, and he laughs out loud when he sees it etched on his friend's face.

"Yeah, my gramps is hanging around here somewhere. So is Uncle Rex."

Riggs's expression goes flat at the mention of Rex. Jimmy laughs again.

"Yeah, if I was sporting a fucking afro like yours, I'd be nervous around Uncle Rex too. He has been holed up

193

here for almost a month now, and I bet he is still shiny bald." Jimmy rubs his bald head and snickers.

"Man, he is gonna call me a sorry excuse for a skinhead," Riggs says while tapping himself a smoke from his pack. Rex has known Riggs his entire life, and most of the time, he is calling him a sorry excuse for something. Riggs tells himself it is all in fun, but it has worn very thin since he has become the man he is today. Rex is unashamedly cantankerous and habitually violent, so Riggs does count himself lucky for only collecting a little verbal abuse over the years. He recalls many instances of Jimmy bearing the scars of Rex's wrath: broken noses, blackened eyes and an eternally lumpy forehead. Rex may have been maniacal in general, but he was fanatical in his support of a Nazi worldview. For a three-hundred-pound man covered in low-quality prison tats and sporting a shiny bald dome, he had charisma to rival Hitler himself. Jimmy and Riggs grew up watching him whip crowds of people into murderous mobs. They also grew up watching Rex practice what he preached with ruthless abandon.

Jimmy stands up and climbs into the back of the truck. He rifles around in his bag and pulls out a couple of Maglites and a single propane lantern. He tucks a semiautomatic pistol in his belt and swings an SKS over his shoulder.

"Damn, Jimmy, why do you still need the hardware?"

194

From the back of the truck, Jimmy smiles his reptilian grin and cocks his bald head.

"You still thinking this is about a little robbery, Riggs?"

Riggs's shock is authentic. "It's not?"

"No. This is about destiny. Let me tell you about my Gramps." Jimmy hands Riggs a flashlight and a handgun. Riggs tucks both in his pants, and they pick up the case.

Jimmy walks backwards out a side door to the garage Riggs hadn't seen before. They enter a stairwell that—with the exception of the Nazi propaganda spraypainted all over—is in much better condition than the rest of the building. Jimmy nods at the graffiti and smiles.

"I did this when I was fourteen. One of the first times my old man and Rex brought me out here."

"Your Gramps has been here for decades?"

"Shit, Riggs, Gramps has been here since right after World War Two. In fact, Gramps was a scientist for the SS. When the Reich fell, he raided the lab for the super-solider serums they had been working on in order to prevent the lowlife Jew servants from getting their filthy paws on them. As he was searching through the lab, the allied forces attacked. They're dropping bombs and shit on the base, and Gramps is risking his life to save experiments done in Hitler's name. Buildings exploding, tanks rolling over razor-wire fences, and Gramps is jumping over halfblown-up bodies instead of hiding."

They navigate the case up the first flight of stairs. Jimmy sets his end down and takes one last drag from his cigarette. He exhales all the smoke out his nose so he looks like a coiled dragon in the dim glow from their flashlights. Small bits of glowing ash drift to the floor as Jimmy grinds the cigarette into the wall next to him. He shines his flashlight up the next flight of steps, checking for obstacles. Satisfied nothing will trip them up, Jimmy grabs his end, and Riggs does the same. Jimmy walks slowly up the stairs, purposely making Riggs wait to hear the rest of the story. He looks at the walls and nods as if he is saying hello to old memories, avoiding Riggs's impatient glare until they reach the third-floor landing. When Jimmy does make eye contact again, he laughs at Riggs's expression.

"Calm down," Jimmy waves at Riggs, "I'll finish the fucking story."

Riggs digs a wavy cigarette out of a crushed pack in his front pocket. He nods for Jimmy to continue while he tries to smooth it back into something straight enough to smoke.

"So Gramps made it to the lab, but he only had time to grab one out of two cases," he gently kicks the side of the metal case they just moved, "before the building comes down in rubble. Forever silencing some of the most advanced research into gene splicing, the occult, amputation and prosthetic weapons, torture and interrogation ... shit, man, all kinds of dark shit. He was ducking in for the second case as the bomb hit. The Allies took his legs at the knees, but he crawled through a slaughter to safety."

Riggs deems his cigarette ready and lights it. "So what was in the case your Gramps grabbed?"

"The fuck-ups."

"Wha ...?" Riggs almost laughs, but the look on Jimmy's face tells him now is not the time for jokes.

"Yeah, Gramps grabbed the case full of the failed experiments and serums." Jimmy rubs his head with one hand and shines the flashlight beam on the wall, revealing even more spraypainted messages and symbols of hate. Deep gouges outline the simple swastika and SS lightning-bolt graffiti.

"Gramps found himself a nice quiet town, and he did what brilliant Aryans do. He continued his work. Most of the documents with the failed serums were incomplete, and even more were lost in the journey from there to here, so Gramps had to figure out what was what by trial and error. Good damn thing there was this little town off the beaten path and filled with foolish American test rats."

"Your Gramps was a scientist for Hitler, he lost his legs in an explosion trying to save his experiments, all that I can believe. But if you are gonna stand here and tell me he killed this whole damn town, I'm gonna call your bullshit, Jimmy Scissors."

Jimmy scoffs at his friend. He holds a finger up to his lips. Total silence grips the building. Riggs realizes for the first time that he doesn't hear the sound of birds outside in the warm spring afternoon. The wind wails as it blows through the decaying building. And something creaks loudly in the darkness behind Jimmy. As if he was waiting for the sound, Jimmy shines the light over his shoulder in the direction from which it came. Riggs jumps back and pulls his gun when the light shines on a pale, legless monster leaning on muscular arms and watching them from the darkness with three eyes. A swastika is carved across its wide chest. The pink of the scar tissue stands out against the alabaster white of its flesh. The beast growls at them and then turns and crawl-slithers away.

"He made help." Jimmy laughs. All the color has slipped from Riggs's face, and heat rises from his chest and neck as panic wraps tight around his mind. He points his gun at the darkness, much too shaky to successfully hit anything, breathing hard and blinking fast. Jimmy laughs again.

"You want to carry the big gun, little boy?" Riggs looks at the SKS Jimmy is offering and nods. "No fucking way; it's my gun."

"These things know me." Jimmy motions towards the case, signaling the end of break time. "I've been around them my whole life. And you can cram your 'bullshit' right up your ass, because Gramps did wipe out this entire damned town, smartass. One by one, and then once he had used the finest specimens to make the first of his super-soldiers, well shit, that's when things got fun."

"So those things are the townspeople?" Riggs asks around the crooked cigarette clenched between his teeth.

"Yeah, there are only, like, three dozen left living. Gramps rigged this place with sound and played constant recordings of Hitler's greatest speeches while they twitched and convulsed on the filthy basement floor as the serum changed them. The transformations turned out to be a much longer and more hazardous matter than Gramps had hoped. Entire families died during the change. The successful ones would end up eating the failures. The strong consumed the weak. However, even the strongest amongst them can't handle direct sunlight for more than a moment or two. Their skin can stop bullets, but it blisters and peels in under five minutes."

The two skinheads enter a big open room on the third floor. The ceiling looks to be the most secure on the floor, even featuring an unbroken skylight. The far wall has two windows, each on either side of a doorway. Whatever was once through the door has fallen away, and the treetops sway what looks like mere feet away. Cream-colored tile walls the room, and most of it remains, despite large cracks extending from ceiling to floor. Smack in the middle of the room, a high-backed wheelchair sits unmoving. The steel from which it is constructed shimmers in the sunlight cast from the skylight in stark contrast to the filthy, damaged floor. The chair looks brand new.

Jimmy leads them into the room, where they deposit the case next to the wheelchair. He pulls another smoke from his pack as the clatter of shattering glass echoes from the far corner of the room. Riggs turns toward the sound and realizes it emanated from an elevator shaft in the far corner of the room. He takes a step but freezes when he hears wet ripping sounds and low growls from the shaft as well.

Jimmy smiles at Riggs and tells him, "Two down, two to go."

Before Riggs can even make his questioning face, Jimmy holds his hands to his mouth and shouts, "Gramps, I got the case!

## CASPER AND SETH

The sound of shattering glass slices through the gloom of the back side of the crumbling building. Casper pulls his gun at the sound, and Seth almost passes out. Casper looks at the skinhead, the runt of the gang, and shakes his head.

"What?" Seth spits.

"Nothing. What's your problem?" Casper lowers his gun but doesn't tuck it back into his pants.

"That was probably just Dennis getting drunk enough to fall down. Maybe he fell through the floor in this shit hole." Casper chuckles nervously.

Seth ignores him and walks into the bathroom to which Jimmy directed them. He shivers in the sunlight blasting through the shattered window. The bathroom looks to be in better shape than the rest of the first floor. All the walls are intact, and there is only moderate flood damage to the carpeted floor. The smooth metal above the sink still casts a slightly warped reflection back at Seth as he rubs his skinny fingers nervously over his bald head. Casper follows Seth in and drops the sacks of cash into the rusty sink.

"You'd better get a hold of yourself," Casper snarls.

"Yeah, yeah, 'cuz after you and your zealot friends arrest Jimmy Scissors, everything will be just hunky fucking dory for me, huh?" Seth says to Casper while watching his reflection warp and stretch in the makeshift mirror.

Casper rolls his eyes.

"Or you could whine a little louder, and Jimmy can come on down here and teach us why they call him 'Jimmy Scissors,' you stupid bastard."

Casper has been working undercover to infiltrate Jimmy Scissors's gang for going on two years now. Seth has been an informant for four years. A DNA test cornered him hard and fast in the rape case of a twenty-year-old black girl. Seth knew that if he didn't work with the cops, Jimmy would kill him for hearing what he did. His family would suffer for his sins. Seth agreed to help the police as soon as they got the offer out of their lying lips.

So far, in that four years, the only thing he has done to keep himself out of prison is vouch for Casper. They only had to bring Casper in once Seth proved himself every bit as ineffective an informant as he was as a criminal. Casper hates Seth, but he has to be nice because, after all, Seth holds his life in his hand. Seth knows the biggest secret in Casper's life, and Seth's mood swings and increasingly erratic behavior have been giving the undercover agent a bad case of nerves.

"What does it matter?" Seth yells, and Casper backhands him into the corner of the small bathroom. He sinks a knee into Seth's gut and then slaps him in the forehead hard enough to snap his bald head back into the wall behind him. Seth crumples, and Casper presses the barrel of his gun into the side of Seth's head. The metal slips on the layer of nervous sweat, so Casper digs it in a little.

"Shut your fucking mouth, you pile of shit. I've worked too hard to bring this sicko and his merry family of murders down for too damn long to have a dipshit like you go and screw it up."

Tears glaze Seth's eyes as warm spittle from Casper's mouth splatters across his pale face.

"All right. Shit, Casper. I'm just freaking out here. Maybe tell me 'Everything is gonna be all right, Seth' or

'You ain't got shit to worry about, Seth.' You know, something."

Casper pulls the gun away from Seth's forehead, and a drop of sweat falls from the barrel. He stands up and tucks the gun into the waist of his jeans. Not regulation, but it is how the thugs do it, so it is how he does it.

"I wish I could tell you any of that, Seth. But the hard truth is we are in this until we see Rex Haas or until they figure us out and kill us." Hearing the words out loud makes Casper wish for a swig off of Dennis's whiskey. He is scared as shit. The dilapidated safe house in an abandoned town, the bloodbath of a job (dead cops, dead robbers, and dead civilians), the metal case covered with German and United States government decals, and Jimmy's strange behavior since this morning are all adding up to a screaming ulcer in Casper's gut.

"I got a bad feeling here, Casper," Seth whines as he stands back up and wipes away a mix of fear, sweat, and tears. "Something don't feel right here."

"Listen to me, Seth. We just got to wait 'til we see Rex. Then I'll send the text I've got waiting on my phone, and this entire damn nightmare will be over. I need you to get your game face on here."

Seth nods and tugs the bathroom door open. He takes a step out of the sunlight, into the dark hallway. He takes another step before something white swoops down from above and yanks him into the darkness. A fan of blood splashes across Casper's face as Seth wails in pain.

Casper hesitates before leaving the bathroom, and in that instant, he sees a monster swinging from the exposed beams above them. The creature releases Seth from its claws, and he is flung like a rag doll into the remains of a wall. Weakened by years of neglect and weather, the sheetrock crumbles to a gray dust, clouding the room. The dust burns Casper's eyes as he stalks blindly toward the sound of Seth's gasping and gagging.

Seth realizes something is wrong as soon as he hits the wall; he just doesn't know what it is. The blood gushing out of his neck with every beat of his panicked heart demands most of his attention. Casper reaches him and tries to tug him back to his feet, but the length of rebar sticking out of Seth's abdomen holds him brutally in place. Casper doesn't realize this, and tugs Seth harder and harder. Seth gurgles blood as he attempts to beg Casper to leave him alone to bleed out. Casper tugs again, and Seth screams in agony. Seth raises his gun with a shaky hand and levels it at Casper.

Casper is vaguely aware of noises surrounding them in the wreckage of the hallway, but the barrel of Seth's gun hypnotizes him. Casper sees his life flash as if it is projected from the tip of the Desert Eagle pointed at him. He thinks to himself that he deserves this bullet.

Bang!

He exhales sharply and then breathes in quickly, filling his lungs with the stale wall dust. A creature behind him squeals furiously but crawls toward them with two thick arms. It drags its torso with amazing speed, hissing and snarling as it closes in. Casper faces the approaching abomination just as Seth fires three more shots at it. The first shot swings wide and clips the doorway to the bathroom. The second hits the creature in its chest but doesn't slow it at all. The third bullet strikes the monster right next to its third eye, giving it a momentary pause. It coils backwards, shakes its horned head, and then continues its charge.

In the flash from each shot, Casper sees the other monsters working their way toward them. Some crawl, some cling to the walls and defy gravity, and a few swing from the beams above. All bear thick pink scars of Nazi symbols and three eyes. Each also has thick horns curling down from the crown of its forehead, ending in blunt or broken tips. Casper dives through the wall as Seth empties his clip at the hideous creatures. He slips in the muck on the floor, giving the monsters time to reach Seth. He doesn't have enough strength to scream or fight and is torn apart in seconds.

After devouring Seth, the creatures duck or smash through the ruined wall after Casper. Sunlight sneaking out from cracks in the boards over the windows casts an eerie half-light into the hallway. The crawling ones duck the beams of fading sunshine. The creatures swinging from above deftly maneuver around them. Casper fires a few hopeless shots at the monsters before he raises his gun and fires half a clip into the fragile ceiling. The tactic works, and the ceiling collapses down onto the unholy monsters.

Casper chuckles at his luck and pulls the cell phone out of his pocket. As his thumb hovers above the send button, with a gotime message to his unit, a monster leaps, snarling, from the wreckage. Casper doesn't have time to backpedal, and the thing's horns crack against his skull. The two fall in a heap but break through the weak floor and crash into the basement. They land with bone-shattering impact as the other monsters swarm the massive hole left in their wake.

**RIGGS**

"What the hell do you mean 'two down, two to go'?" Riggs's confusion warps into a nervous feeling that rumbles his stomach. He has known Jimmy Scissors long enough to know that if he wasn't made part of the real plan, it is because he wouldn't have agreed to it.

Jimmy turns to him, scowling, and shushes him.

"Shit, man." He looks around the room, paranoia sparkling in his blue eyes. "I meant my crew was a joke. A cop, a rat, and a couple of queers. Rex would kill me if he knew, so I brought them here to help them disappear."

"What?" Riggs says louder than he means to, earning another threatening glare from Jimmy.

"Shit, Riggs, for a white man, you sure can be ignorant," Jimmy scoffs. He looks around again before continuing. "Dewayne and Dennis were gay for each other. Seth got flipped and brought in Casper, a mother-fucking undercover cop. This is an Aryan brotherhood, not a disco bar or donut hut. If word had ever gotten out, the Hammer would have killed me. So I fixed the fucking problem."

"So everyone else is dead?" Riggs asks, still trying to wrap his head around Jimmy's revelations.

Before Jimmy can answer, the deafening clatter of gunfire echoes ominously throughout the decrepit building. The floor below groans, and monstrous growls intermix with the rapid gunfire. The entire building rumbles when a large chunk of ceiling collapses from the second floor to the first. The growls resume, but the gunfire does not.

"I'd say so," Jimmy says. He turns and looks his friend in the eye. "And no one ever needs to know about this. All right?" "Yeah," Riggs nods distractedly.

"Besides, today it all comes true. Today, my Gramps's vision of an Aryan master race is realized. Hey, are you listening to me?"

Riggs hears Jimmy, but the voice in his head telling him to run is even louder. *Too deep,* he thinks. He didn't see any of this coming, and it really fucks up his plan. He was hoping to pull this job and then bail. He had found reason to first doubt, then despise what Hitler's Hammer was really all about. Everything about which Jimmy has suddenly felt so conversational only confirms his feelings. At the same time, it takes away his paddles and kicks his raft down Shit Creek. If Jimmy has already eliminated everyone else, he'll have no qualms about one more. Riggs cracks his neck and turns to Jimmy.

"Yeah, shit," Jimmy chuckles. He stifles his laughter quickly, and his mood sobers. "Now listen. Gramps is a little different. Not as different as the crawler you saw earlier, but different. If your life means anything to ya, don't stare at the old man. Got it?"

*Too deep, too fucking deep,* Riggs thinks. He says, "Got it."

The silence after the booming gunfire and collapse is high pitched and pure. Riggs is content to let it squeal in his ear, but Jimmy just keeps talking.

"No more small-time shit, Riggs. This is the beginning of the Final Reich. We begin world domination tonight, brother. We have the working super-soldier serum in this here box. We will be generals of an unstoppable army! We will be the super-soldiers the Fuhrer dreamed of, leading the Aryan race into the future with our heads held high. The master race will rise and conquer! Heil Hitler!"

Riggs is lost in a nightmare. Jimmy's face is flushed, and there is a twinge of fear hidden deep in his blue eyes. The sunlight stabbing past the trees and through the open door and windows is dying, and the room takes on a jaundiced tint. Riggs doesn't answer. He feels the weight of his Desert Eagle tucked in the back of his jeans and wonders briefly if he could kill Jimmy and escape the monster he had seen earlier. Sensing Riggs's distraction, Jimmy takes a step closer. Riggs sees the fear mixing with confusion, and he knows that paranoia will follow. He opens his mouth to repeat the slogan, despite how it tugs at his nervous gut.

A loud creak from the corner of the room steals both men's attention. A shape moves in the shadows, and a deep, wheezy laugh wraps around the room. The shape takes a molasses-slow step forward, and a smile worms its way across Jimmy's face as he steps away from Riggs to face the darkness.

"Heil Hitler!" a voice chants back as Rex staggers from the darkness. A frail-looking old man is clutched tight to his back, with his arms around Rex's mammoth neck. Two purple tentacles twitch and sway from behind Rex as he stumbles forward another step. Rex raises his head sluggishly and regards Jimmy and Riggs with the slightest of nods. Riggs takes notice of the poorly bandaged stump where Rex's left hand used to be and the faraway look in his eyes. Jimmy steps to the side so Rex can carry Gramps to his wheelchair. They reach the chair, and Rex leans down slowly. Jimmy reaches over, and Gramps grabs his shoulder with a bony hand as Jimmy helps him.

The old man stretches once in his chair, reaching his frail arms high into the air above him. The purple tentacles sway back and forth from where his legs should be. They wrap and unwrap around the cool metal of the high-backed wheelchair. Riggs notices the old man is, indeed, very old. Long snow-white hair hangs off his head in clumps. His skin is pockmarked and so thin that Riggs can see black and blue liquids running through veins just below it. He has a headset with a microphone attached to it, and he adjusts it before turning his attention to Riggs.

"Heil Hitler," Gramps says in a calm yet devilishly threatening voice that makes his body seem less frail. In the depths of the building, a growling chorus chants, "Heil Hitler" so loudly it reverberates throughout the building. Jimmy stands rigid and snaps his heels together. He raises his hand toward Gramps and returns the chant. Even Rex, who sways slowly in place with his eyes distant and clouded, stands straighter and raises his stubbed arm to mumble his own "Heil Hitler."

With three dangerous members of the Haas family all staring at him, Riggs salutes and repeats the words. "Heil Hitler!"

Gramps leans back in his wheelchair and smiles his rotten grin at Riggs.

"Did you know," Gramps asks Riggs in his husky voice thick with German accent, "people used to cry in the streets when they said this?"

Jimmy flexes his muscles and cracks his neck. Rex stares at Riggs with eyes tinted red and gold. Fear forms a lump in Riggs's throat, and he can only shake his head.

"They felt such admiration for the Fuhrer that they could not control their tears. The people cried tears of joy." The smile fades on Gramps's face. His face goes slack,

210

but the skin remains taut. His leg tentacles sway and point at Riggs. "And now we shout it in abandoned buildings in a rabid Jew country. Say it with pride, always."

Riggs feels the underlying threat in the advice, and he nods his understanding. Jimmy scoffs softly to himself as he leans down to break the lock on the metal case. Rex stares through Riggs as much as he stares at him. Jimmy is proven wrong, as Rex's head hasn't seen a razor in weeks. Tufts of sandy blond hair point in every direction from atop Rex's massive cranium. The big man sways softly in place, almost in unison with the old man's tentacles. The bandage covering his stump is filthy; thick black goop stains it and oozes from between layers of wrapping.

The lock on the case snaps, and Jimmy tosses the lid open. Gramps claps his leathery hands together. "After all this time," he sighs.

Jimmy pulls out a thick folder and hands it to Gramps. The old man flips through the papers, talking— sometimes laughing—out loud but to himself. Every now and then, he taps Jimmy on the shoulder and points to a glass vial within the case. Jimmy takes the vials and lines them up on his shirt, which he has laid across the filthy floor. After nearly a dozen are out, Gramps turns to Rex, who is still staring at Riggs, and says, "Give me the kit, Rex."

Without taking his distant, empty eyes off of Riggs, Rex digs a small black satchel from a pocket of his torn and bloodstained flannel. He holds it out, and Jimmy reaches up and grabs it. Rex's arm slowly drops back to his side. Jimmy opens the case and revels three large hypodermic needles and two halfempty vials. The liquid in each is the color of weak iodine, whereas the vials lined up on the floor are all clear. Rex trembles and takes a slow dragging step backwards when he sees the open kit.

Gramps frowns, and Jimmy scoffs again. Gramps scowls at Jimmy before pointing at a vial on the floor. "That one is for Rex."

"And now we can fix you up, Rex. Stick that stump over here so Jimmy can help you."

Fear awakens in Rex's eyes, and he shakes his head back and forth slowly. His cheeks wobble around his open mouth as drool drips from the corner.

"It is okay, Rex, you've been brave," the old man reassures him. "Let Jimmy get you healed. You will be the first of the new breed."

Rex drags his feet away from Jimmy, but Jimmy is quick for a musclehead, and he grabs Rex around his good wrist. Rex tugs his hand to his chest, and Jimmy is nearly pulled off his feet.

"Grab him, Riggs!" Jimmy screams as Rex jerks his arm and a struggling Jimmy back and forth. The distant look returns to Rex's eyes, and he looks like a bear playing with a toy. Out of instinct, Riggs follows Jimmy's command and wraps his strong arms behind Rex. Once he can't move, Rex looks around slowly to see what is stopping him. He turns and looks over his shoulder and sees Riggs straining to hold him in place. His eyes cloud over as he makes eye contact.

"Now!" the old man barks.

Jimmy digs the needle into Rex's bandaged stump and injects the fluid from the vial. Rex howls in pain and flexes his massive upper body. As he swells, the pressure on Riggs's elbows proves too much, and he loses his grip. Rex backhands Jimmy away from him with his good hand and tosses an elbow at Riggs's head. Both men hit the ground and bounce right back up. Riggs tackles low and Jimmy clotheslines high at the same time but from different directions. The big Nazi crumples, and the floor cracks visibly when the three men crash into it. The serum flowing through Rex's veins grips him and seizes control of his muscles. His body jerks and kicks while he groans and spits frothy green foam all over himself.

Jimmy backs away quickly, blood trickling down from a broken nose over two badly split lips, and turns to Gramps. The old man points to a door opposite the elevator shaft. Jimmy nods. Riggs stares at Rex convulsing on the floor. Jimmy reaches over and gives Riggs a forceful nudge. Riggs shakes away the voice inside that just keeps repeating *too deep* and looks at Jimmy. The skinhead nods at his uncle, then at the room at which Gramps pointed. Riggs doesn't say anything, but he leans down and grabs Rex's good arm around the shoulder. Adrenaline pounds in Jimmy's ears, and the only way he has ever dealt with it before is to fight, but he realizes the stakes and grabs Rex's other arm. The two men drag the behemoth across the floor, past a smiling Gramps in his wheelchair, through the dying rays of sunlight retracting to the windows.

They drag him all the way into the room, sitting him against the far wall. Rex's eyes have rolled back in their sockets, and blood and a thin black slime drips from his ears. He gurgles once and tips over, smacking his head hard on the floor before he resumes convulsing.

"Where is your head, brother? This is the realization of the dream!" Jimmy whisper-shouts at Riggs.

"Shit, Jimmy, this is a fucking lot to take in. Why didn't you tell me everything? Shit, you didn't tell me anything."

"If I had told you I was gonna kill everyone, what would you have said?"

The voice inside answers, but Riggs ignores it and says, "I don't know, Jimmy. But I'd have some time to adjust to the fact that our crew is gone and that, after tonight, we are taking over the world with a batch of monsters."

Before Jimmy can speak, Gramps's voice booms throughout the building in German. The monsters hiding in the shadows howl and crawl toward their leader. The building creaks as the creatures crawl through the hallways and swing from the ceilings. Jimmy and Riggs walk back toward Gramps, who is still shouting German into the microphone. He smiles as they approach, and his tentacles reach for them when they stop. He motions behind them, and they turn to see a dozen of the crawlers crowded in the dark room behind them. The two in front hold Casper by his arms. Most of his flesh has been peeled off, but he still groans softly.

"You see," Gramps explains to Riggs, "because of their previous exposure to the serums, we can only give the soldiers certain serums, and we can't inject them, because their flesh is much too hard for the needles." The two monsters drag Casper to Jimmy. He stabs the cop in the face with a hypodermic needle and injects a full vial of serum. Casper's eyes fly open. He tries to scream, but his throat is too damaged. Jimmy loads a second vial in the needle and stabs it into Casper's face again. Once the needle is empty, he snaps to attention and signals to his grandfather,
"Sieg Heil!"

The creatures all repeat the phrase in gravelly inhuman voices. Gramps salutes them back and yells it into the microphone, "Sieg Heil!"

The monsters holding the now-convulsing Casper jerk him to the elevator shaft, and all the others follow. They disappear down the shaft, howling and repeating "Sieg Heil" over and over again like excited idiot children.

Riggs watches the monsters vanish and stares at the vacant shaft. He hears them begin feasting, and the voice tells him, *Now! Now is your chance!*

Jimmy loads up another vial and prepares to shoot himself up. Riggs is standing behind him and, since Jimmy

215

is leaning down, he can see Gramps. The old man stops Jimmy with a touch on the arm. Jimmy looks up, and the big black swastika on the back of his head blocks Riggs's view. The old man tells Jimmy softly, "Your friend first."

The voice in Riggs's head screams, *NOW!*

Riggs pulls his Desert Eagle and aims for the center of the swastika. The bullet hits its target and explodes out of Jimmy Scissors's forehead. Bits of skull and brain matter splatter all over Gramps's face. Jimmy's lifeless corpse slumps to the floor, leaving a scant few feet between Riggs and the old man. Gramps grins, and a third eye opens in the middle of his wrinkled forehead. Riggs aims at it. The bullet hits its mark as well, and the old man's brains spit out behind him in a geyser of crimson and gray. Riggs shivers once and runs back down to the van.

He is talking to himself and hardly notices the smell of gasoline as he runs through it on the second-floor landing. He throws open the door to the garage, ready for his freedom. Instead, he is shot in the chest three times and falls back onto the gasoline soaked carpet.

**BEN**

Ben didn't like what he found behind the curtain in the garage. The first thing he noticed were the hundreds of shoes hanging from the high ceiling. Some had fallen and lay, moldy and rotten, scattered around the dirt floor. Rex Haas's custom painted '87 Volkswagen van was parked at a crooked angle, pointing into the corner. The thin layer of dust coating it indicated that no one had driven it for a while, meaning Rex was most likely around there somewhere. Rex knew Ben's girlfriend was Mexican, and he didn't try to hide his disdain. Ben knew firsthand how violent Rex and Jimmy could be, so he did his best to keep a low profile around the Nazi thugs. He shook off disturbing memories and walked around the rear of the van, taking note of the missing rear window and the obvious bullet holes. He opened the door and choked down the vomit that had been trying to rise all morning. A thick black-and-brown stain covered the entire cab of the van and was smeared across the windshield. The sound of Dennis's whiskey bottle shattering in the basement echoed loudest on the first floor. Ben got scared then.

He shut the door as softly as he could. On his way back to the other side of the curtain, he noticed jars of small bones, frail and yellowed from time, sitting on a tall wooden table against the wall. The vomit finally had its way.

Ben slunk back through the curtain and noticed the other bags of cash hadn't moved yet. He decided to see what everyone else was doing. He heard the gunshots seconds before he opened the garage door. The sound of the ceiling collapsing and the hungry growls that followed convinced Ben he didn't need to wait around. Instead, he thought he'd call his girlfriend and tell her he was coming home with a little something extra. He noticed he had a few new messages. He knew who they were from, but what they were saying didn't make any sense. When he closed the cell phone, he realized he had grabbed his girlfriend's phone by accident. Ben's anger was meaner than his fear.

It took him less than twenty minutes to siphon the fuel out of Rex's van. It took him another ten to douse the entire first floor and a little of the second with the siphoned gasoline. He found Dewayne's Desert Eagle in the back of the moving van as he was shutting the doors and readying to leave. The confident weight of the weapon convinced him to go back for the other bags of cash. He was reaching for the door when Riggs jerked it open.

Now he stares down at the man he just shot three times. Riggs chokes down a massive gulp of toxic air, coughs up thick brown blood, and stares back. The fumes blur the air around Riggs, and his eyes are having a hell of a time staying open.

"I'm so sorry," Riggs cries.

Mercy aims the gun at Riggs's head instead of his balls.

"I'm so sorry. I'm so sorry, Maria." Riggs weeps loudly. "Maria, I'm so sorry."

The words vanquish mercy, and Ben pulls a matchbook out of his front pocket. He strikes one and sets the book aflame. He stares through the flame at Riggs, who is still apologizing to Maria.

"Nazi asshole," Ben says as he drops the flaming book onto Riggs's gas-soaked crotch.

The flames roar to life instantly and devour the rotted walls and floors greedily. Ben ducks away from the blaze and runs to the van. It starts on the first try, but when Ben shifts it into reverse, something big barrels out of the flames and into the side of the moving van. The big vehicle rocks from the impact, but Ben holds the gas down, forcing it out through the closed wooden doors. As the rear of the van is splintering the garage doors, three heavy green tentacles slap against the windshield. Ben panics and crashes into a pile of stacked cars twenty feet out of the garage. He shakes off the crash and notices where the tentacles came from.

Rex walks slowly toward him as the garage behind him is engulfed in flames. A half-dozen tentacles wave from where his left arm should be. His old eyes are glazed over in a shiny reddish gold, but he has other eyes, all bright blue, staring ravenously at Ben from his cheeks, chin, and forehead. His jaw dislocates, revealing three rows of jagged teeth. Another mouth opens in the middle of his throat, yet another on his shoulder.

Ben steps on the gas and cranks the wheel hard to avoid the mutated Nazi. Rex lurches forward, and tentacles shatter glass. Ben screams once before they wrap around his throat, silencing him forever. He doesn't make any more noise, but he feels it when the tentacles around his neck drag him through the broken window. His last thought is of decayed broken teeth goosestepping across piles of deformed human carcasses.

# THE SELF-MUTILATION BLUES

*It's a suicide note you can dance to, baby.*

I woke up this morning to fog drifting through my living room and a song stuck in my head. In a world where words hurt, these ones strangely soothed me and set my scars atingle. My toes tapped air, and I broke my own rule by getting up before noon.

*It's a suicide note you can dance to,*
*baby,    that pain that gets us through.*

A smile found its way onto my face. It was weird, but I decided to just go with it. The forward momentum of motivation jerked me into my morning routine. The smile itched, and I almost lost the song to a random thought about bloodstains—how they taste and fade.

*It's a suicide note you can dance to,*
*baby,    that pain that gets us through.*
*When you're bleeding, you're never alo-oo-ne.*

I stood in front of the mirror, naked so I could berate myself out loud. I keep track of my failures by carving X's on myself, and I look like I'm wearing a fleshy plaid bodysuit. I traced the heart-shaped scar on my chest with a trembling finger and pondered the future.

*It's a suicide note you can dance to,*
*baby,   that pain that gets us through.*
   *When you're bleeding, you're never alo-oo-ne.*
    *A pound of flesh will pay your dues.*

Next, I felt hope, I think, because my normally steady fingers were jittery as I removed my razor blade from my necklace. I dug the blade into the scar and dragged it along the heart-shaped outline as I had so many times before. Maybe this time would be different, maybe this time, I could feel. The unscarred flesh inside the heart turned red as the disfigurement burst open in the razor's wake. The cut was perfect, and I felt my blood—warm and sticky—flowing down my stomach. I felt nothing inside. I'd failed, yet again, but I had no more room for X's. My smile did nothing but mock me. Good thing I can sing without lips.

*It's a suicide note you can dance to,*
*baby   that pain that gets us through.*
   *When you're bleeding, you're never alo-*
*oo-ne.       A pound of flesh will pay your dues,*
    *Oh, yeah, baby, it's the self-mutilation blues.*

# TEMPER LIKE A HAMMER

He is fighting now. He doesn't recognize the men he is hitting and kicking. Each kick is an exercise in determined antagonism because of the murky thigh-deep swamp battleground. Each strike is the simultaneous euphoric rush of satisfaction and gutwrenching need to release as knuckles pop and split against faces and skulls. He doesn't recognize the men pulling his hair and attempting to strangle him. The furious cries and curses of unbridled rage ring through the air, dozens of different languages and dialects twisting into a maelstrom of irate resonance.

A man with a two-toothed snarl under a handlebar mustache slugs him in the chest with both hands. He feels his ribs crack as he rocks backwards. His breath speckles his attacker's face with warm blood as he passes to smash another man in the ear. He kicks the chest-puncher just below the kneecap. The man stumbles one step away from him before he collapses into the riotous brawl. He decides against following the man; his broken ribs stabbing into his lungs and stomach make even the slightest movement excruciating.

His agony steals his anger. The pain calms him enough for guilt and shame to flood in its place. As his fury dissipates, the storm of voices muffles as if he has plunged into the water. He refuses to fall, as to fall would be to admit his anger. His mistakes. His faults. His sins. His anger returns a hundredfold, and he leans forward with it, smashing a man in the face with his forehead. He feels the man's nose shatter flat against his skull and shoves him underwater and beneath the feet of the other violently brawling men. His splintered bones stab at his punctured organs, but it all grows numb beneath the intensity of his anger. The screams of pain and fury around him return in full volume as he digs his thumbs into the eyes of the next man he can reach.

## X

Officers Bret Nolan and Bradley Marsden work their way up the tenement, stepping over the trash that litters the hallways, both with pistols drawn. Their target, Miles McVarney, is hiding in a room on the fifth floor. As they reach the fifth floor, the sounds of rap music boom from behind a closed door so loudly that the men must choose to either shout at each other or rely on hand signals they have worked out during their time as partners. The only lighting in the hallway comes from dim bulbs overhead, the light diluted further by the cheap glass light fixtures under them. The two men are stalking forward eyeing the door to Miles's apartment, when a door between them flies open and two crackheads, one male and one female, spill out into the hallway.

Both crackheads notice the men, with their pistols drawn, and know immediately that they are cops. Nolan and Marsden cast disapproving glances at the wasted pair but make no move to arrest them. Instead, Nolan holds his finger to his lips and continues past them, focused entirely on the door hiding Miles from them. The crackheads plaster themselves against the hallway wall and watch with twitching eyes as the cops navigate the trashed hallway. As Marsden approaches them, his eyes carry an unspoken warning to remain silent. Then his eyes dart to the woman's pale, thin legs. His glance is slow and deliberate, cold and dangerous as he examines the jittery and scantily clad woman.

The song thudding in the background ends. The weak glow from the overhead 50-watt bulbs flickers casts the hallway in quick flashes of shadow. Another song starts with a deep bass groove that rattles the walls. The vibration also shakes loose one of the overhead light fixtures and drops it to the floor, where it shatters into hundreds of yellow-tinged shards. In the same instant, the male crackhead screams at the top of his withered lungs.

"Mutha' fuckin' po-po! Fucking po-po in the hallway!"

Nolan casts a furious glance at him, but the butt of Marsden's gun silences him when it cracks so hard into the man's forehead that the back of his head dents the cheap drywall behind him, spilling dust all over. Two doors open at the exact same time: the door to Miles's apartment right in front of Nolan, and a door behind them, which releases the rap music full force.

Miles dashes out of his apartment, casts a quick frightened glance to the two officers, notices the hulking gangbanger with the semiautomatic hand cannon and black-and-red Atlanta Falcons jersey emerging behind them, and smiles a graveyard grin at the cops before continuing his escape. Nolan's vision tints red as his temper bubbles over. In his mind, the only living thing in the hallway, in the world, is a quickly fleeing Miles.

Marsden grabs the formerly shouting man, now only half-conscious thanks to the well-aimed pistol-whip, and with a firm tug throws him at the wickedly armed gang-banger. The gangster responds by suppressing the trigger and letting loose a hail of gunfire, reducing the tweeker snitch to a twitchy mass of pulp and sinew. In one swift move, Marsden grabs the woman by her hair and forces her back through the doorway she had just exited with his left hand. At the same instant, his right hand fires two quick shots that hit the giant gang-banger in his forehead. The bullets tear out the back of the big man's head, shredding his red bandana and splattering thick crimson chunks all over the hallway walls.

Nolan chases Miles opposite the carnage and gunfire to the stairwell leading to the lower floors. The

226

black trench coat Miles wears flaps behind him as if it mocking Officer Nolan through the flickering lights. Miles dares a glance behind him as he approaches the stairs, a glance that demonstrates his confidence slipping away as fast as his chances of escaping the furious form of Officer Bret Nolan. The cop is two steps behind him as they reach the top stair. Officer Nolan dives to cover the short distance, tackling his prey down the short flight of stairs to a landing in between the floors. Miles's body absorbs the weight of both men as they crash awkwardly into the wall before crumbling to the floor.

Miles manages a few gasps of stale-smoke air before the cop punches him in his face, shattering bone, blackening both eyes, splitting his upper lip, and knocking three teeth down Miles's throat. The takedown and follow-up direct hit take the fight out of Miles quicker than a tazer would have, and he weakly waves for mercy.

Bret Nolan shows him none.

His anger has overtaken him now. He sees everything in a red tint. The white floor is pink. The pale yellow wall is the color of mango skin. The blood dripping from Miles's ruined nose is black. He mumbles words at the criminal, but the froth in his mouth muffles the curses and pools in the corner of his lips.

He clenches his fist and hits him again. And again. And again.

He sees purple bruises bloom across Miles's exposed skin like flowers of pain. He feels fragile face bones rend and separate under his solid knuckles. Miles attempts to cover his face and head, so he drops a knee onto his crotch in order to get a few more shots in. Miles howls in agony, but Nolan hears only whispered whimpers as he cracks Miles's jaw with another knee strike. He raises his fist, but Marsden pulls him off the quivering beaten form on the stairway landing.

"Easy, bud," Marsden tells him in a calm, non-combative tone of voice. "If we kill him, we can't ask him any of the questions we need to ask him."

The red drips from Officer Bret Nolan's vision like blood trickling from Miles's face as his anger slowly fades. Marsden holds him against the wall and allows his partner a few deep breaths before continuing.

"I've got a two-dead clusterfuck up here that I'm gonna have to call in. As is, it's gonna be another two hours before we can even talk to this shit bag because of the paper work I've got to do now because of the two chunks of scumbag bleeding all over the shitty carpet up there. It'll give this one some time to get stitched up in case you need to kick his ass again. You cool?"

Nolan says nothing. His cold unmoving eyes are locked on the semiconscious Miles. His breaths are still deep, each releasing anger like pressure. After a few more of these deep cleansing breaths, Marsden asks again, with a whisper of force tinting his tone, "Are you cool?"

Nolan turns his eyes to his partner, only the faint slivers of anger residue glimmering, and nods. Marsden smiles and pulls his hand away from Nolan's chest slowly. The walkie-talkie clipped to Marsden's belt crackles the silence to shreds. He offers his partner a knowing smile and disappears up the stairs, reporting his account of the shootout to the person on the other end of the walkie.

Officer Brett Nolan tugs the plastic zip ties the police carry instead of the old-fashioned handcuffs from his belt. He hogties a moaning Miles in a quick, brutal fashion, squeezing and twisting as much as possible. He stares at Miles, helpless and beaten on the blood-streaked floor. The anger flares once, a random burst of fury, and he stomps the bound man's head against the floor.

## X

Hours later, after completing the mountain of paperwork and plethora of interviews that come with discharging your weapon, Officer Marsden finally joins his partner in the small room adjacent to the interrogation room where Miles sit slumped in a folding chair. Marsden wonders silently how long Officer Nolan has been staring at Miles through the one-way glass. His partner's face is slack and emotionless, almost detached in its calmness. Marsden sees no hint of the rage he saw hours before until he looks in Bret Nolan's eyes. There, fury bubbles and rolls in the dark orbs focused entirely on the beaten man hunched over the table in the next room.

Needing his partner to show considerably more restraint within the confines of the police station, in a room wired with sound and video, Marsden clears his throat and draws Nolan's attention. Marsden watches the anger drift away in his partner's dark eyes like a ripple in calm waters.

"Yeah, I'm cool," Nolan grumbles. "I know this mother fucker knows something about *her*."

Marsden has spent years studying the human condition, and he recognizes the way his partner emphasizes the last word of his sentence. There is something personal about the disappearance of the young woman, Shannon Nellson, which Nolan isn't sharing with him. It doesn't matter, of course, because Marsden has already seen the rage in Bret Nolan, and he has made special note of it. No sir, you couldn't hide such a deep fury from Officer Bradley Marsden.

Nolan keeps staring at Miles through the glass for another couple of minutes before he finally notices his partner hasn't gotten up to begin the interrogation. Marsden just smiles a knowing grin at him while leaning against the table holding the cache of video-recording equipment.

Nolan returns the grin with a shadow of a smile, the best he can muster while suppressing the murderous intent inside him.

Marsden speaks though his grin. "Are you sure? If we are going to have any chance of finding this Shaley girl-"

"Shannon," Nolan corrects immediately. Marsden detects something else in his tone along with the anger, but he can't quite put his finger on it. Regret? Remorse?

"Right, *Shannon*," Marsden continues, perfectly aware of his mistake. "If you go cracking this guy around anymore, not only will he not tell us anything, but he'll likely sue the holy living shit out of us. We can play 'good cop, bad cop' if you want. I'll do the talking, and you just sit there and give him that crazy eye you've been giving him from here."

"Okay." Nolan nods and opens the door. Marsden smiles to himself as his partner walks out of the room. Before he leaves, he reaches back and pulls the main power cord to the recording equipment. The screens instantly shrink into blackness. Marsden watches through the glass as Nolan walks into Miles's room. The criminal almost pisses himself.

Bret Nolan walks into the room, and Miles's eyes go wide with fear—well, the eye that isn't swollen closed goes wide with fear. Miles scans the room quickly, as if looking for an escape hatch he hadn't previously noticed. Nolan's eyes never leave the panicking Miles, and the fury in them never wanes, despite the man's wordless entry. His anger is a physical presence in the room, a pressure behind his eyes and pushing against Miles's thin chest. Miles's eye watches Nolan as he sits down, flexing his arms and chest menacingly. Nolan's face is emotionless other than the intensity burning in his eyes. He only stares straight at Miles.

Miles begins weeping and blubbering under his glare. "I don't know nothin' about her! I just know she's running from something, I don't know what or why or where the hell she ran off to."

At the mention of "her," Nolan's muscles flex, his hands curl into fists, and he leans forward as if to stand. His vision tints the familiar red, and in the instant before he loses control, Officer Marsden eases into the room like he was carried on the breeze. Marsden puts one hand on his shoulder, and Nolan leans back with a creak but doesn't take his eyes off Miles.

"It's okay, Miles." Marsden tells him in a voice so calm one wouldn't think he had been a part of a bloodbath just a few short hours before. "We just want to talk. If you don't know anything, why were you running?"

Miles wagers a quick one-eyed glance at Officer Nolan and shivers. "Because he was chasing me! His eyes were crazy! Look, they are fucking crazy now! This guy wants to kill me!"

Nolan says nothing. His eyes grow wider. His vision grows brighter and redder.

Marsden snaps his fingers to get Miles's attention as if he were a misbehaving child. Miles turns away from Nolan, who is beginning to tremble with the rage building within him, to face the far less threatening Officer Marsden. Bret Nolan continues staring at the side of Miles's face.

When the other cop and the criminal start conversing, Nolan hears them muffled under his heart pounding in his ears. Their voices are distant, almost like underwater whispers. He stares at Miles's face—the long stubble-speckled jaw, the swollen eye facing him, and the nose he smashed flat a few hours ago. His vision glows in reds and pinks. He is glaring at the side of Miles's face, but now the criminal's words are completely silent as his mouth pleads with Marsden and he repeatedly shakes his head "no" in response to other, equally mute, questions.

Nolan realizes he is leaning forward. He suddenly feels doubt. Maybe Miles really doesn't know anything. Maybe the scumbag is telling the truth. Maybe she didn't tell him where she was going. Doubt leads him back to regret. Redder vision responds to the regret as his anger flares more forcefully than before.

He is leaning forward when two eyes open in blinking unison on Miles's battered cheek facing him. A bulb of flesh swells under the eyes, like a flapping fleshy tumor on Miles's neck. It slowly bobbles into the shape of Miles's crooked nose.

Across the length of Miles's neck, a smile curls from the skin, spreading flesh-colored lips to reveal black and broken teeth. The morbid face steals his anger and replaces it with shock and disbelief.

233

His red vision drips away, and the second face speaks to him. "She is never coming back."

Nolan's eyes tear at the words. The unmistakable feeling of regret slashes through his heart. He mouths the word "no" to the face on Miles's neck. The neck-face laughs, a sound like rails screeching.

"You know she isn't. You did this. You know you did. Your temper, your fault."

He is breathing deeper now. His world tints red, darker and deadlier than before. His hands clench into hammer-hard fists. The face on Miles's neck notices him losing his temper while Miles continues whimpering and pleading to Officer Marsden, blind to Nolan because of his swollen eye.

The neck-face smiles at him and mocks him in a singsong voice, "Your temper, your fault, your temper, your fault, your temper, your fault." As Nolan's lips curl into a snarl, it speeds up, sensing the coming attack.

He shoves the table aside as he charges. Miles turns to face him, and fear drains the color from his real face even as the face on his neck continues screaming. He ignores Miles's real face and swings hard at the mouth on the man's neck. Fist meets jaw and cracks on impact. The force of the blow tips Miles backwards in his chair. Nolan rears back for another strike, but the echoing racket of gunfire thunders inside the small room as Marsden puts two bullets in the falling Miles. One in his heart and one in the exact same spot Nolan's knuckles just shattered. By the

234

time Miles crashes to the floor, he is dead, missing most of his face from the nose down, and the face on his neck has disappeared.

Bret Nolan turns and stares at Marsden. The solid highpitched ring from the gunfire ensures continued silence from Marsden as his mouth moves in angry, easy-to-read curses. Nolan doesn't know how to respond, so he says the only thing he ever says, despite its utter meaninglessness: "Sorry."

Marsden shakes his head and sticks a finger in his ear. Then gives it a good wiggle so Nolan understands he can't hear shit either. Marsden reaches into his back pocket and pulls out a switchblade knife. He hunches over Miles and grabs his hand. Next, he uses the dead man's hand to trigger the blade from the knife. Still holding the knife with Miles's fingers, Marsden tosses it across the room toward a shocked, pale Nolan. Wearing the same knowing grin as before, Marsden mouths words to his hothead partner. "I just saved your life."

Nolan still doesn't know what to say. Marsden leans in so he can speak straight into his ear. Even as close as he gets, he has to shout. "You tell them he pulled a knife and dove toward you. I busted two quick caps in his ass." Officer Nolan nods his understanding. Before backing up, Marsden shouts, "And meet me at the apartment across from Miles's apartment tonight at midnight." Nolan gives him a questioning look, but Marsden mouths the words "you owe me" as the room floods with other officers responding to the clatter of gunfire.

## X

He is fighting now. His face is swollen, lumpy, and bruised dark greens and purples—a parody of its former self. He wears a dripping crimson mask birthed from deep gouges in his forehead. Someone has bitten off most of his left ear. His lips are split and fat like grave worms. They bleed down his lopsided chin when he bellows curses at the other fighting men.

He throws a reckless elbow behind him, cracks an unseen enemy, and then throws all of his weight forward to smash his head into a staggering man's face. His victim responds with a gut shot that speckles his face with blood. Then the victim offers a head butt of his own. He staggers away from the onslaught only to be tackled almost in half by another rag-clad and bloody man. Pain flares up his side as more ribs break from the impact. A few previously broken ribs are ground to sharp barbs that tear at the nerve clusters up and down his spine. Both his legs go numb, then scream with intolerable pain that loosens his tough-guy bladder.

He is getting tired. His hands are heavier and therefore harder to lift. He bleeds from nearly every exposed part of his body. Every breath, every slight movement reveals new bone fractures and torn muscles.

236

He tastes bile, blood, and snot. Red bubbles tease at his nostrils, quaky as his breath. His innards seep and rupture like mush in a bruised skin bag. Yet, still he fights, punching another man in his throat hard enough that his fist feels the man's spine with his split knuckles.

He spins next and wraps his arm around a man's neck. Long blond hair, clumped with blood into small dreadlocks slaps him in the face as he squeezes his anger out. The blond man struggles and begs. He hears nothing. He sees the blond hair but doesn't know who he is strangling. A sudden panic creeps up his crooked spine. Blond hair. His fear makes him angrier, and he squeezes the blonde's neck harder to compensate.

He feels shame. And he squeezes harder. He feels regret. And he squeezes harder.

The blonde goes limp in his arms, the fight choked out. He doesn't let go of the corpse. He doesn't want to let go. Even though it was his fault.

## X

Officer Bret Nolan is walking up the same stairwell he stalked with his partner hours before. He assumes he will meet Officer Marsden upstairs, but he doesn't know why. He knows he let more of his anger show than he intended to, and he knows Marsden picked up on it. Bret Nolan has had a temper his entire life, and very few who saw it got the chance to tell others. Throughout his life, he has lost his temper often. However, his ability to cry on cue has always transferred the role of victim to himself. Very few people can turn a cold shoulder to a man whimpering and crying, with snot dripping off his chin, when he threatens suicide to combat the monster within. He perfected his own victim routine so well that his victims were often ignored in the wake of his tearful performances.

He realized during his late twenties, as people were beginning to see the pattern of temper to victim, that he either needed to seek professional help or hide his monstrous anger better. Both proved nearly impossible, as he simply couldn't hide his temper, and dealing with his anger only brought other feelings (regret, guilt, and self-loathing) to the surface, and were feelings he wouldn't allow himself to experience. They would put the blame for his actions back on him and, of course, that was not an option. He only lost his temper when someone pushed him. It didn't matter that begging for mercy would set him off or that anyone, even those closest to him, were at risk of his selfish violence. What mattered was never being to blame for his actions.

These realizations led directly to his choice of career. Now he doesn't need to hide behind his tears, because he has a shiny brass badge to hide behind. He found that few people questioned officers of the law, especially when their brutal methods yielded a high arrest rate. Even fewer questioned the bruises and cuts the criminals wore after dealing with him. He was a well-respected member of law enforcement, and no one questioned him.

Until this morning, that is. Marsden somehow knew there was something different about this missing persons case, and Bret Nolan suspected his partner knew it was something personal. He doubted that Marsden knew why he was so interested in finding Shannon Nellson or that he suspected him of any fault in her sudden disappearance. Still, Marsden had twice in one day covered for his furious temper, so he felt bound by a strange form of camaraderie to honor Marsden's wishes and return to the scene of Miles's arrest.

These thoughts keep him distracted as he turns onto the fifth floor. He makes note of the dozens of red footprints that crowd the hallway from people walking through the puddles of blood left by the two dead men earlier in the day. He ignores the blood and brain splattered on the walls. He barely notices the strands of yellow police tape covering the door to Miles's apartment. He makes slight note of the thudding rap music, blaring as loud now, at midnight, as it had at ten in the morning, behind the door that released the gun-toting gangbanger. But his attention is drawn instead to the door the two crackheads exited before causing the murderous chaos that followed. He hears noises seeping into the deserted hallway. As he reaches to push it open, it moves inward of its own accord.

Marsden stands in the apartment and invites him in. Marsden has abandoned his button-up shirt and blue tie for a black leather g-string with leather straps connected at a ring in the center of his muscular chest. His surprise at Marsden's outfit doesn't last long, as the fresh bright-red scratch that splits the man's cheek and forehead demands his attention.

"Jesus, Brad, are you okay?" Nolan asks, worry and confusion tinting his voice.

Marsden dismisses his worry with a nonchalant wave of his hand. "Yeah, yeah. Don't worry about this little scratch. Kitty gots claws, I'll tell you that."

"Huh?" Is all Nolan's reeling mind can offer.

"I'm glad you made it, partner." Marsden chuckles and invites him into the filthy apartment. Used fast-food wrappers and discarded hypodermic needles litter the entire floor. "I thought you would, but you never can tell."

Again, Nolan says, "Huh?"

Marsden chuckles a second time, an unnerving grating sound. "I saw it in your eyes twice today, man. The anger and the fury you try to hide so well."

Nolan's eyes grow wide, and his stomach clenches like that of a junkie in need of a hit. All he can think is: *He knows*.

Marsden sees the look of worry on his partner's face and chuckles yet again. "Don't worry, man. I understand."  "You do?" Nolan asks, his confusion blooming.

"Sure do, man. I feel it too," Marsden confides.

"The anger?"

"Oh, yeah. The anger and the frustration. I feel it as well. Hell, I bet most of the people we work with feel it too, but they are too weak to do anything about it. We stand on the front line, dealing with the dregs of society and the filth they inflict upon good, hardworking people. And I'm here to tell you, we need a release from them. We need a way to vent our furies, or they will get the best of us. That's why I wanted you here tonight."

Before Nolan can spit another "huh" into the room, Marsden leads him through the trashed living room to an even more torn-up bedroom. Marsden hold the door open, and Nolan walks in. His eyes are immediately drawn to the skinny woman, naked and handcuffed to the twin-sized bed. Her face is a beaten, lumpy mass with two panicked eyes darting back and forth between Marsden and Nolan. She whimpers behind the panties stuffed in her mouth and fights weakly against her bonds.

"I brought her in here after her little boyfriend tried to get us killed this morning. The bitch slashed my fucking face when I turned her back over for you-"

"Why?" Nolan interrupts.

"Because, this little waste of skin will never be missed. Because she deserves everything she gets. Because crime is wrong, and criminals need to be punished. However, dragging her to court and then to jail would only be a drag on the people. The people we are paid to protect. So we take out our frustrations on her for her kind. We are the law, brother."

Marsden pats him on the back and shoves him toward the frightened bound woman. He gestures to a metal tray with several knives, clippers, and other sharp instruments of torture; several of which have thin strands of crimson flesh hanging off of them.

"I've already had some fun with her." At the words, Nolan notices the growing puddle of blood spreading out from underneath the woman's ass cheeks. "After you give her a little pounding, we can get down to the serious business of law enforcement the way it should be."

Marsden smiles at Nolan, but Nolan has too many thoughts swirling through his head to put words to them. Marsden misinterprets Nolan's stunned expression and tells him, "Ah, hell, sorry. You need some privacy to get it up. I don't blame you. I'll just give some of these tools a good cleaning while you do your thing."

He grabs the metal tray and walks out of the bedroom, whistling to himself. Nolan looks to the woman. Tears stream down her cheeks, dampening the fresh bruises and cuts on her face. She begs for his mercy, and he understands her words even through the cotton clogging her mouth. *This isn't right,* Nolan thinks. He leaves the woman and sneaks out of the room. He hears her cries of relief as he stalks into the disgusting kitchen.

Marsden stands at the kitchen sink, rinsing the morbid tools of the flesh clinging to them. Nolan opens his mouth to speak, but two eyes blink open on the back of Marsden's head, just under his buzz cut. A nose wiggles free, and an evil grin opens up right above his partner's neck. Bret Nolan freezes in place and makes eye contact with the face staring back at him from the back of his partner's head.

The mouth opens and begins speaking, rendering Marsden's whistling a muffled whisper. "You should turn right back around. Now is your chance to release that anger that ruins everything for you. How many people has it pushed away? How many lives has it ruined? Take it out on that little whore. Teach her a lesson. She needs it."

"No," Nolan tells the face.

Marsden turns half around and notices Nolan. "Damn, done already? You must've had more pent-up sexual fury than I thought. Give me just a minute, and we can get down to the real business." He then turns back to the sink and the task of cleaning the implements of pain.

The face on the back of his head speaks again. "What do you plan on doing? Killing me? Well, hell, you might as well. Because you know that, no matter what, I'll figure it out sooner or later. I'll know everything about Shannon Nellson soon enough."

Nolan draws his gun at the mention of the name and points it at the back of Marsden's head.

The face scowls and continues. "Do you think that'll help you find her? You know she's never coming back. Your temper, your fault."

"No!" Nolan screams and pulls the trigger. Marsden turns as he yells, and the bullet hits him in the side of his head. It exits the other side, coating the wall with his pulpy gray matter. He slumps to the floor, his twitching feet kicking garbage about as he dies.

"I'll find her," Officer Bret Nolan tells his partner's lifeless corpse. He watches Marsden's postmortem twitches and tells the body, "I'm not like you. I'm not sick. I'm nothing like you. I'm not a monster."

He leaves Marsden's body and returns to the woman in the bedroom. Her eyes are wide after hearing the gunshot, and when Nolan walks in, his gun swaying at his side, tears of relief flood her eyes. Nolan reaches down and tugs the gag out of her mouth.

"Oh, thankgodhewasgonnakillme. Thank you, mister, thank you."

"Shhhhhh," Nolan comforts her, "it's gonna be okay now." He reaches over and finds the binds holding her down to be tied far too tight for him to untie. He curses under his breath and tells her, "I'll be right back. I gotta get something to cut these." She pleads for him not to leave, and something in her voice grates on his nerves. "I told you, I'll be right back."

He leaves her sobbing form and returns to the kitchen. He grabs a knife off the counter and heads back to the bedroom without looking at Marsden, his odd leather outfit, and the growing puddle of his blood. He returns to the bedroom and freezes in the doorway.

The woman is still lying prostrate on the bed, but two brown eyes have opened under her small pert breasts. A nose has risen just under her sternum, and it flares its fleshy nostrils at him. A smile opens on the emaciated stomach, revealing shiny white teeth where intestines should be. Even stretched and horrid as it is, he recognizes the face. When it speaks, its soft sweet voice muffles both the sirens rising in the distance and the woman's muffled pleas for help.

"I'm never coming back. You know I'm not. What you did is unforgivable."

Bret Nolan's eyes go wide with righteous fury, and his mouth goes dry. His vision tints the warm, familiar red. His teeth clench and grind. His fists shake, and his stomach rolls.

"You did this," the face on the woman's stomach tells him. "Your temper, your fault."

Bret Nolan grabs the one torturous tool Marsden hadn't used yet: a brand-new framing hammer. He picks it up and feels the cold weight in his hand. The woman is crying as he steps closer, his eyes betraying his intent. He spins the hammer in his hand and raises the clawed end above his head. He will never accept the blame. It is easier to lose control than to admit what happened. The hammer falls, and the woman's cries of agony echo through the apartment building.

## X

He realizes all at once that the blonde is dead. He has choked the life away, yet his anger still rings in his ears. He is sinking. The weight of the corpse is dragging him down. His hands are heavy. His heart is heavy. He tries to let go of the blonde's neck and when he does, he sees her face. His guilt overwhelms his anger, and he sinks below the murky surface of the water. As the dirty water fills his lungs, he speaks words that turn to bubbles as they float toward the surface.

"My temper, my fault."

# THE DEVIL'S BATH SHACK

The trees have been known to calm me, yet they haven't since that day. I was walking off a fit of rage when I came upon the shack. I stumbled into a hillside clearing, and there it stood in all its wooden one-room malevolence. A creek rushed silently beside it, the underwater blades muffling its flow. Demons and birds perched in the surrounding trees, watching me silently with glowing eyes and rotted souls.

I would have walked away and sought my masochistic redemption in the thick dark of the woods, except I heard the theme song from MASH from inside the little structure. The song was sorrowful, but the jokes immortal. Hawkeye could always cheer me up, and Klinger wore dresses my mother emulated. She never smiled as much as he did, though. Flower-patterned funerals have a different taste. I pulled myself from my memories and pushed the door open without knocking.

My poor-manner karma was instant and uncomfortable. Splinters dug into my fingers and squirmed under my fingernails.

I thought of sweet January—naked flesh, bloody lips, shivering in summertime. The song changed, and I found myself tapping my foot on the dirt floor to Rezso Seress's "Gloomy Sunday." A twosong soundtrack for students of sorrow.

A demon stood on a stepstool, the song emitting from his wide-open mouth. He held a sign that read, "Gunmetal Tastes Like Cherry" scrawled in black Sharpie. I marveled at his musical innards reproducing such a haunting tune. A tear formed in my eye as the song reminded me of failures and aborted dreams.

"Why do you disrupt my bathing?" a calm deep voice asked from behind me.

I turned and noticed a man sitting in an old stand-alone bathtub with hooves instead of rounded feet. The man had two small horns protruding from his forehead and a bubble beard. Rose petals and eyeballs floated on the surface of his steaming bathwater. A black dog with mismatched eyes curled up on the dirt floor next to the bathtub. I thought of sweet January again— her lovely scars and gnashing teeth. The horned man snapped his fingers. My memory vanished in the echo.

"Why do you disrupt my bathing?" the man asked again as his soap beard dripped.

The music stopped, and I looked back to the demon. He glared at me and held up a sign that read, "Razor Blade Rebellion." In the silence of the shack, I missed the haunting tune. I shrugged and mumbled an apology.

"Is there no common decency anymore?" the man asked.

The black dog raised his head and shook negative.

The demon started the song over from the beginning, and my toes tapped along. He held a sign that read, "The Tighter the Noose, the Sweeter the Juice" scrawled in black marker. I found courage in the pit of my stomach, where all the bad feelings swirl, and used it to answer the bathing man.

"No," I told him, "for everyone burns in the fire of life."

The horned man splashed his bathwater at me, flinging eyeballs and rose petals all over the floor. The water hit my face and plugged my nose. My eyes burned, but I told myself I'd never cry in front of strangers again. You never know if the strangers know we are all ghosts in the fog. So it's better not to give them the chance to judge you.

"I see," the man told me while applying more bubbles to his chin. "And what of forgiveness? Does it still pester?"

"No," I told him, "for solitude is a cold, flaming mistress."

"I see," he answered. Then he pulled a rag from the water, held it out to me, and asked, "Could you wash my back?"

"No," I told him, "for I lost my kindness when all my toys broke."

He nodded sadly and lost himself in his own memories. I shuffled my feet and waited impatiently for him to speak again. The black dog stood slowly and stretched, one eye on me and one eye on my nightmares. Still, his master said nothing. So I broke his concentration by snapping my fingers. The echo wasn't nearly as impressive, but still he looked at me.

"May I steal your demon?" I asked, using the voice I employed when I'd asked for the toys—now broken— when they were shiny and new.

The horned man leaned back in his bath and slid down into the water. He opened his mouth and swallowed up bathwater, then spit it out like a fountain.

"No," he told me, "but you may take his sign if you wear it around your neck."

"Fair enough," I answered, content to leave the humid room with my soul and a souvenir.

The demon handed me the sign with a small loop of barbed wire attached so I could wear it. I put it over my head and bowed. The horned man waved me away. The black dog scoffed and spun in place three times before lying back down beside the bathtub. I walked out the wooden door into the night.

My eyes glowed strange neons as they led me home through the forest. Demons and birds squawked and chirped blasphemies at me, but the words on the sign kept me strong. I held a sign for all to see that read, "My Emotions Are Zombie" scrawled in black Sharpie.

JONATHAN MOON

www.ingramcontent.com/pod-product-compliance
Lightning Source LLC
Chambersburg PA
CBHW021226130626
46554CB00004B/1384